DIARY OF AN OXYG

ANONYMOUS

Also by Anonymous

Chameleon in a Candy Store

DIARY OF AN OXYGEN THIEF
ANONYMOUS

corsair

CORSAIR

First Corsair edition published in the UK, 2016

34

Copyright © 2006 by Anonymous

The moral right of the author has been asserted.

A CIP catalogue record for this book
is available from the British Library.

ISBN: 978-1-4721-5275-6

Printed and bound in Great Britain by Clays Ltd, Elcograf S.p.A.

Papers used by Corsair are from well-managed forests
and other responsible sources.

Corsair
An imprint of
Little, Brown Book Group
Carmelite House
50 Victoria Embankment
London EC4Y 0DZ

An Hachette UK Company
www.hachette.co.uk

www.littlebrown.co.uk

For Matty

DIARY OF AN OXYGEN THIEF

ANONYMOUS

1.

I liked hurting girls.

Mentally, not physically, I never hit a girl in my life. Well, once. But that was a mistake. I'll tell you about it later. The thing is, I got off on it. I really enjoyed it.

It's like when you hear serial killers say they feel no regret, no remorse for all the people they killed. I was like that. Loved it. I didn't care how long it took either, because I was in no hurry. I'd wait until they were totally in love with me. Till the big saucer eyes were looking at me. I loved the shock on their faces. Then the glaze as they tried to hide how much I was hurting them. And it was legal. I think I killed a few of them. Their souls, I mean. It was their souls I was after. I know I came close a couple of times. But don't

1

worry, I got my comeuppance. That's why I'm telling you this. Justice was done. Balance has been restored. The same thing happened to me, only worse. Worse because it happened to me. I feel purged now, you see. Cleansed. I've been punished, so it's okay to talk about it all. At least that's how it seems to me.

I carried the guilt of my crimes around with me for years after I stopped drinking. I couldn't even look at a girl, much less believe I deserved to converse with one. Or maybe I was just afraid that they'd see through me. Either way, after getting into Alcoholics Anonymous, I didn't even kiss a girl for five years. Seriously. Not so much as holding hands.

I meant business.

I think I always knew deep down I had a drinking problem. I just never got around to admitting it. I drank purely for effect. But then, as far as I was concerned, wasn't everyone doing the same thing? I started to realize something was wrong when I began to get beaten up. My mouth always got me into trouble, of course. I'd go up to the biggest guy in the place and look up his nostrils and call him a faggot. And then when he'd head-butt me, I'd say, "Call that a head-butt?" So the guy would do it again harder. The second time I'd have less to say. One of my "victims" stuck my head on an electric cooker ring. In Limerick. Stab City. I was lucky to get out of that house alive. He'd done it, though, because I'd been taking the pith out of hiths listhp. Maybe that's why I moved on to girls. More sophisticated, doncha know. And girls wouldn't beat me up. They'd just stare at me in disbelief and shock.

Their eyes, you see.

All the pretense and rules dissolved away. There was just the two of us and the pain. All those intimate moments, every little sigh, those gentle touches, the lovemaking, the confidences, the orgasms, the attempted orgasms—all mere fuel. The deeper in they were, the more beautiful they looked when the moment came.

And I lived for the moment.

I was working freelance in advertising all through this period in London. As an art director. A contradiction in terms if ever there was one. It's what I still do today. Strangely, I was always able to get money. Even in art school, I got a grant because my dad had just retired and I suddenly became eligible. And after that I got job after job without too much trouble.

I never looked like a drunk, I just was one, and anyway in those days advertising was a far more boozy affair than it is today. Because I was freelance, I could be my own man, so to speak, and I would keep myself busy by ensuring I had dates lined up. None of the girls were supposed to know this. The idea was to have an impressive queue so that when one girl neared maturity—usually after about three or four dates with some phone calls in between—another would be introduced. Then as one went onto the scrap heap, a new one would take her place. Nothing unusual about my method, everyone did it. But I enjoyed it so much. Not the sex or even the conquest, but the causing of pain.

It was after my crazy night with Pen (more on that in a minute) that I realized I had found my niche in life. Somehow I was able to lure these creatures into my lair. Half the time I was trying to push them away, but it had just the opposite effect. And the fact that they were attracted to a piece of shit like me made me hate them even more than if they'd laughed in my face and walked away. As for looks? I'm nothing special, but I'm told I have beautiful eyes. Eyes from which nothing but truth could possibly seep.

They say the sea is actually black and that it merely reflects the blue sky above. So it was with me. I allowed you to admire yourself in my eyes. I provided a service. I listened and listened and listened. You stored yourself in me.

Nothing had ever felt so right to me. If I'm honest, even today I miss hurting. I'm not cured of it, but I don't set out to systematically dismantle like I used to. I don't miss the booze half as much. Oh, to hurt again. Since those heady days I heard an adage that seems to apply here: "Hurt people hurt people."

I see now that I was in pain and wanted others to feel it, too. This was my way of communicating. I'd meet the women the first night and get the obligatory phone number and then after another couple of days, making them sweat a little, I'd call and be all nervous. They loved that. I'd ask them out and pretend I hardly ever did "this kind of thing" and say that I hadn't been out a lot in London because I didn't really know the scene. This was true, though, because all I used to do was get out of my head in local bars around Camberwell.

We'd agree to meet somewhere. I liked Greenwich, with the river and the boats and of course the pubs. And it had a great boyfriend/girlfriend feel. Nice and respectable. I'd be half out of it before we even met, but I'd be witty and charming and boyish and shaking. Trying to put me at ease, they'd smile and comment on my trembling, thinking I was nervous to create a good impression. Because I wasn't getting in enough booze, my very being would shudder. I'd have to order two large Jamesons at the counter for her every half lager. I'd down the Jimmys without her seeing and then on with the show.

Lovely.

I didn't really care if I got them into bed or not. I just wanted some company while I got pissed, while I waited for the courage to hurt to well up in me. And they seemed pleased because I wasn't trying to grope them. Sometimes I would. But mostly I'd be fairly well behaved. This would go on for a few dates. In the meantime I would encourage them to tell me about themselves.

This is very important for the successful moment later. The more they confided and invested in you, the deeper the shock and the more satisfying the moment at the end. So, I'd be told of their dog's habits, their teddy bear's names, their father's moods, their mother's fears. Did I like kids? How many brothers and sisters did I have? A sitcom I had to sit through. But it was okay, because I knew I'd be writing her out of the series.

She'd talk and talk and talk, and I'd nod. Raise a strategic eyebrow. Grimace when necessary. Guffaw or feign shock, whatever was required. I'd watch people in conversation and record their facial expressions. Interest: Raise one eyebrow and raise or lower the other depending on the conversation.

Attraction: Try to blush. Not easy, this (thoughts of what I was going to do to her later helped). And a blush usually begot a blush. That is, if I could muster a blush, she was more than likely to blush back. Sympathy: Crinkle the forehead and nod gently. Charmed: Cock your head to one side and smile apologetically. I'd supply these prefab masks on cue. It was easy. It was enjoyable. Guys did it all the time to get laid. I did it to get even. Unkind to Womankind. That was my mission. Around this time I discovered the meaning of the word "misogynist." I remember thinking it hilarious that it had "Miss" as a prefix.

All I know is, I felt better when I saw someone else in pain. But of course they would often hide how much I had hurt them. Yes, it was a challenge in itself to help her externalize her feelings, but also bloody frustrating to have gone to all that trouble and then not be able to enjoy a dramatic playback. That's why it became necessary to condense everything into the one demonstrative moment.

Sophie was from South London. She used to do the wardrobe for Angus Brady on the comedy show *Aren't You Glad to See Me?* I met her at a Camberwell College of Arts party that I had crashed. After her, there was that designer girl—whose name I honestly can't remember—who I'm sure I hurt very deeply because she never called me back. Funny that, because even though I never met her again or even heard her say another word, I knew she had it bad.

How do I know?

I know.

There was Jenny. She was the one who threw the beer in my face. I was thrilled to have had a hand in causing so much rage.

Then came Emily. But she doesn't really count because she was as good if not better at whatever this is than I was. I kind of fell for her. Laura was somewhere in there. An ex–band publicist with a superb arse that had survived a young daughter. I woke up one morning and there was an eight-year-old girl watching as I tried to extricate myself from the freckled tentacles of her comatose mother. And then after she guilted me into walking her to school, I got the feeling that mother and daughter made full use of the men that passed through their lives. Like the Native American and the Buffalo, The Eskimo and the Seal, The Welfare Mother and Me.

And the one who started it all.

Penelope Arlington. I'd been going out with her for four and a half years. Long time. She'd been nice to me. Nicer to me than any other girl had ever been. When I spoke, she turned her head toward me and seemed to abandon herself to the meaning of my words. I liked that. It was only much later that I found out she was terrible in bed. At the time I thought she was wanton. She wasn't. But she's the one I regret hurting the most. Why? Because she didn't deserve it. Not that the others did, but she wouldn't have left me if I hadn't ripped her apart. And I needed her to leave me because she was getting in the way of my drinking.

And one night I just cracked up. It'd been bubbling for ages. Simmer, simmer, bubble, stew . . . gurgle. I got completely fizzingly drunk and this whole chain of events began to rattle. Why would anyone set out to break the heart of someone he loved? Why would anyone intentionally cause that kind of pain?

Why did people kill each other?

Because they enjoyed it. Was it really that simple? To achieve a soul-shattering, it is better if the perpetrator has been through the same experience. Hurt people hurt people more skillfully. An expert heartbreaker knows the effect of each incision. The blade slips in barely noticed, the pain and the apology delivered at the same time.

I had grown tired of the girl I was going out with for four and a half years. I loved her. That was the awful thing about what I'm going to tell you. The possibility exists that she's out there somewhere reading this right now. The rest of you turn your heads away; the next bit is for her only.

Pen, I'm so sorry. I needed to hurt you. I knew we were coming to an end. I knew you had started to despise me. You tried to hide how you felt, but it rippled across your face. Disgust. I began to hate you for not having the courage to tell me what you really thought of me. So I had to make up your mind for you.

The rest of you can look now.

It was a Friday night in a pub in Victoria Park. I was out of work early. Yet another ad agency where yet another clutch of concepts had been mass-murdered by yet another ham-fisted creative director. I was sure of one thing. I needed to get soaringly drunk, so I downed pints of beer at an alarming rate.

The wizened barman seemed concerned. Then whis-key. By 7:30 PM I was stumbling. I was to meet Penelope at eight. I had to walk my bicycle around to where we were meeting. Another pub, naturally.

Anger. Boredom. Drunkenness. A bad combination. I began with something like this: "How can I dismantle four years?"

Her quizzical look was followed by an evasion in the form of "Like my new blouse?"

"Looks. Like. A. Tablecloth."

Hurt look followed by "Another?"

More booze. That would usually work.

"Girlfriend? Yes, please."

Not so much hurt now as bored. Looking around the pub. Silence.

9

Then she said, "Let's go somewhere else."

That would usually work, too. But I'd decided that tonight it wasn't going to. Not tonight. Tonight we were going all the way. This was just the perimeter, the initial sandbags of defense. My svelte band of emotional terrorists skipped mischievously over these insults to their training.

"Sure. Let's go somewhere else."

I resolved to say nothing between this pub and the next. I succeeded. She was trembling now. Unsure. I was trembling, too. From excitement. She ordered some drinks from the bar. Fucked if I was paying for them, and I grabbed a seat at a circular table, over-ogling other girls. She saw me. She was supposed to. Still no reaction. There were four and a half years at stake here. Mostly good. Why wouldn't she allow me one off night? But that's what was so exciting. I'd decided. And she couldn't see what was in my head. The picture of me having sex with that white-skinned, blue-veined prostitute with only one breast. I knew I could cripple Pen. She could probably cripple me, too, but she wouldn't because I was going to do it to her first.

Why, though? I knew it didn't make sense. I did love her in my own way. Very much. She was beautiful and fun and caring, but I was bored, so bored. I had to think of other girls to get a hard-on. I didn't want to start the long arduous road to her orgasm, let alone mine. Afraid to touch her in case it was mistaken for an application for sex. So in order to feel something through the numbness, I decided to perpetrate on my soul and hers the equivalent of quenching cigarettes on my paralyzed limbs. My hope was that if I registered pain, it would be welcomed as a sign of life.

Or maybe I was just drunk.

Either way, my resolve had hardened. "This is what I look like when I'm pretending to listen to your boring conversation."

I froze my sweetest expression, my innocent blues eyes widening in pseudo-interest, the same expression I'd used on teachers. Pen eyed me with suspicion. Here was something new. I turned my face away, like an impressionist readying himself for his next character.

"This is what I look like when I'm pretending to be in love with you."

I gazed at her lovingly but respectfully, the way I had done so many times and meant it. I even meant it now, but only because I wanted it to be convincing.

"Hang on. What else? Oh, yeah. Here's what I look like when I'm pretending you are even slightly witty just so I can get laid later on." And I threw my head back in a guffaw with a head-tilt and a sneaky look out of the corner of my eye. Sorry, girls. Guys know all this stuff, too. She was starting to catch on. Her eyes dulled. I could help her with that.

"And this is me."

This I particularly enjoyed. It had been the catchphrase of Ted Carwood, a very popular British impressionist who'd end each of his shows with that revelation before he bid us good night. It was the one time he appeared as himself. I added a variation. The accompanying expression in my case was one of pure provocation. A mixture of Hit Me and Fuck You that I normally reserved for barroom fights with men much bigger than me. It always worked. I was saying she was a coward if she didn't hit me. She didn't, of course. She just looked at me. Innocently. This was more fun than I'd expected. Shouldn't she at least be crying? I was impressed, if you want to know the truth. But up to this point I was merely doing stretching exercises.

"You think I'm joking. Don't you?"

No response.

"I'm going to dismantle us tonight. And there's nothing you can do about it. You'll have to sit there and listen while I wrench the *u* from the *s*. You'll question your own judgment. Maybe you'll never really trust yourself again. I hope so. Because if I don't want you, and believe me I don't, then I don't want you being happy with someone else when there's any doubt that I might get another girl."

I was not yet aware, you understand, that I was to become the Soulfurnace you see before you. But I was losing the bolt-uprightness I felt I deserved, so I added, "Your cunt is loose."

She heard it but wasn't quite sure how to react. I could help her with that, too.

"Let me put it another way. Your vagina is baggy . . . feels overused."

12

Now we were cooking. Her eyes widened. I saw how she tried to keep her outrage to herself. But it was too late, I was already in there. I could almost see out through her eyes. She couldn't hide. Not from me. I was the undercover cop. I knew all her moves. I'd helped her create them. This was too easy.

"Your tits sag."

This I delivered like a punch. I leaned back to better view the effect.

"They're too big and they hang too low."

This just in case there was any doubt. Shock can protect and lessen the full velocity. Better to be sure you've hit the mark. Mind you, a little confusion is sometimes fun because it makes for wonderful expressions. Often she'll smile at you after delivery of the despicable package, not yet aware of its contents.

"To get a hard-on, I have to think of some girl I've seen on the bus."

I waited for this to sink in. Brought my hand up to my chin as if thinking of the next line. Looked as sweet as I could. I'm good-looking when I'm enjoying myself, or so I've been told.

"By the way, I had sex with another girl other than the one I told you about."

Now I was winning. So I smiled with sympathy.

A winner doesn't want to gloat. Just to win. She looked like someone else, a new person. There was nothing more for me to extract. I wasn't even sure I wanted to hear what would come out. No matter how well chosen the words were, the voice couldn't always be trusted to carry them. Clearing the throat, that was the dilemma. Clearing the throat without letting him know how this affected him. Why was he doing this? Never mind why, the thing is, it was happening.

"Had enough?"

No hesitation. Just one nod of her head. Down and up again. She must have sensed mercy in the air. She sensed wrong. All she'd done was let me know that I was having the desired effect. That she was sobbing inside.

"Yes, well, even so . . . I've done much worse than just have sex with another girl. It's very bad, even by my standards. So bad, in fact, that I'm going to spare you. I might tell you later. I might not. But you would fall apart if I told you, and I'm not sure I want you doing that just yet."

She was so much in shock there was no point in continuing. Did I feel remorse? Not in the least. To further my torture, I inquired about her job and her blouse and her life.

I was careful to utilize some of the facial expressions I had already immortalized so as to inflame her even more. And I seem to remember scrounging some money from her to buy more drinks.

But wait, there's something else. Here's the weird bit. Because I had now given her good reason to take revenge on me, I offered her some options. The keys, as it were, to me. I think this is where I miscalculated.

My logic went as follows: If someone hurts you, then you automatically want revenge. It doesn't matter how long it takes, you want revenge. I thought if I hurt her enough, she would want revenge. Therefore I wouldn't have to worry about never seeing her again. Because that is what I feared most: the fact that I was losing her. The question was how not to lose her for all time. I gave her some hints on how to successfully hurt me back.

Love in disguise.

Never let her know how much you love her or she'll kill you with it. Sadly, though, there is still a little truth in that for me even today. But never mind that. We're talking, Jesus, was it ten years ago?

Yes, I believe it was.

"Call me every night at eight for a few weeks, and when I answer, don't say anything. Make sure there is no music in the background. By the way, I always wanted to fuck your sister; I think she would have gone for it, too. I want you to remember these things I'm asking you to do. I know there's some guy sniffing around you at work. I want you to go away with him for a weekend. Why not? You deserve it. Just go. Don't give me any warning. I won't even remember what I'm saying to you now. I'll probably have a blackout . . . I'll move on to brandy next. That always gives me blackouts. So you'll do it? Good girl. Also, follow me around in your car. Maybe you'll even change your car. You can use Paul as a messenger if you like. You want to be free, don't you? Especially after tonight. Yeah, course you do. Well then, do these things or I'll badger you forever. I'm serious. Maybe you'll only do some of them. That's okay, and you may come up with some of your own ideas and that's fine, too, but I want you to take revenge on me. I want you to hate me. I'm helping you hate me. I'm doing you a favor, setting you free and asking you to do the same for me. Please?"

I had delivered this monologue with as much sincerity as possible. I was in earnest. I wanted her to want to hurt me back. This would be the new *us*: She looked at me. Into me. Those beautiful eyes glazed over all shiny like little blue bruises. And yet she looked stronger than I'd ever seen her. Unattached. Single. Out of reach.

My reach.

It was done. Four and a half years. I had to make sure she would continue to know me. At the same time, I didn't care. I needed something, anything to push me forward. Over the edge, if necessary. I wanted to blame her for what might happen. I wanted to mythologize her. She Who Would Avenge the One Who Dared Rebel.

Romance has killed more people than cancer. Okay, maybe not killed, but dulled more lives. Removed more hope, sold more medication, caused more tears.

Looking back, I see that's what it was: me auditioning for Heathcliff in Hackney. I threw in a few more choice insults—your father is an idiot, your brother is anal, you're not clever enough to be my girlfriend because I'm a genius

16

and I'm tired of pretending to be less clever than I actually am just so you can catch up—and headed off to the bar for brandy. As you can see, I did recall most of the details, but there could well have been more.

For her sake, I hope not.

That night, while trying to eat a kebab, I did fall off my big black bicycle somewhere around Victoria Park. I didn't care if I got up off the tarmac. I was laughing and singing "Born Free" and somehow cycled back to her place later that same night. As usual, she'd left the door open for me.

I remember thinking, "The bitch . . . she hasn't taken me seriously."

But when I clawed roughly into bed beside her, I could feel the vibrations as she cried herself to sleep. I remember her getting dressed the next morning. Writhing into matching white underwear. She was stunning as she stood in front of the mirror. The expression she wore while deciding if she liked how she looked contrasted sharply with what locked into place when she caught me staring at her. I might have been some homeless guy peeping from under those covers.

She went away with that guy from her office. I wasn't prepared for the pain of this. I felt how she must have felt when I hurt her.

You might as well argue with the mirror as argue with each other. After all, aren't we all really the same person?

Anyway, I have this to say. After Pen left, someone did call me at one point every night at eight for about two weeks.

That really freaked me out. I'd answer and . . . nothing. Whoever it was would then gently hang up. The "gently" scared me more than anything else. Passionless. This intrigue suited my paranoid delusions, and my drinking had by now progressed from habit to full-time occupation. It was going to kill me and I welcomed the prospect.

I attributed my misfortune to the guile and cunning of this mousy girl from Stratford-upon-Avon called Penelope. And while I flattered myself that she'd seek revenge, I didn't realize that leaving me to stew in my own paranoid juices was revenge enough. I'd do worse to me than she could ever dream of achieving. When I was nearly sandwiched to death between a car and a motorcyclist, I was able to imagine she'd orchestrated the whole event. I suffered a crushed bicycle and a broken wrist. How delighted I was that she should go to such trouble in the name of romantic revenge against me.

She really must love me after all.

I couldn't piss because my left arm was unusable, and my right was road-rashed. Bladder ablaze, both arms stuck out like I was begging for money from the other would-be patients in the emergency room, and I was smiling. Because Penelope loved me enough to mastermind this attempt on what was laughingly referred to as my life. I fantasized that she would turn up in a nurse's uniform any second and administer a long, slow luxurious hand job . . . but only after she'd helped me take a long, slow, luxurious piss.

Later, I convinced myself that she had turned up at my shitty basement flat disguised as a prospective flatmate. I refused to take this "applicant" seriously. When she asked where the toilet was, for instance, I resisted the urge to applaud. I thought it hilarious that she, having been in the flat hundreds of times, should ask me so convincingly anything about it. She knew more about it than I did, since I was very often in blackout. But I wasn't about to ruin her little sketch. I received each query with a congratulatory smile and answered tongue in cheek. Smiling too broadly and nodding knowingly, I showed the young woman out.

She didn't take the room.

So there's me. My baby'd left me for another guy, who had his own flat, a car, and a coat. I was entering a world of pain, not all of it mine.

Cue the country music.

2.

So now I was ready to pass on my learning to the uniniti-
ated. The unhurt. The innocents. With the girlfriend out of
the way I'd be better able to dedicate myself. I was seriously
pissed off and all I wanted was for others to feel this, too.

Especially girls. A girl had caused it, so a girl would
have to pay. I wanted to hurt. It was a whole new world to
me. I'd never known it was possible to be hurt so much. I'd
been beaten up lots of times and it was nothing like this.

I hadn't expected physical pain. A burning sensation in my
chest as if a large smoldering boulder had somehow lodged
there overnight. A kind of drawn-out, slowly unfolding panic.
The exact opposite of excitement. Accompanying this were
shooting pains running down along the back of my arms. What

was this? Rejection? Was it really this tangible? All I could think about was that if I could be hurt like this, then surely I could cause the same pain in others. This consoled me.

I studied and stored away each new flinch of discomfort. I recorded what had happened and how it affected me. I called and asked her answering machine to hurt me. To be free, I needed to hate her. It was over, but I couldn't bear the fact that I still needed her. So I begged her to hurt me, which she did by refusing to. Meanwhile, I stumbled into London's night in search of hearts to stab.

A teacher from Ireland. Twenty-five-ish. A virgin. No, really. She said I had "an enviable command of the English language." I wasn't sure what I was going to do to her. The answer came to me when I slipped into her bed after cooking my special boned chicken, the preparation of which scared even me because it involved so much tearing of flesh from bone. She was engaged to be married. I hated her for that. It emerged in conversation that being a virgin embarrassed her. She didn't want her fiancé to find her still intact on their wedding night.

I didn't know where to start.

Teach her some filthy tricks that would sow seeds of doubt in the mind of the groom? For instance, I've never thought much of a girl who swallows. Don't get me wrong, it feels fantastic and I'm aglow with gratitude at the time, but only a slut would ever actually do something like that. Not the behavior of a wife-to-be.

Somehow it was obvious that I should leave her virginity intact. It became about him. How to hurt him through her. Anal sex? That would still leave her a virgin. Did she really want to lose her virginity, or was she bluffing? After a huge bottle of wine, most of which I drank from the bottle, I was supposed to sleep on the couch.

This I did until four, when I awoke with a stiffy and slipped in beside her, finding only token resistance. She really did want to lose it. But I didn't like the idea of me as sexual plumber. I wanted to be present on her wedding night. I wanted her body to remember mine the way I remembered Penelope's. I began to lick her out. For two hours. When she became too sensitive I waited and started lapping again very gently.

I looked up now and then to tell her how beautiful she was. I blew cool air on her. I stroked the insides of her thighs and tried to imagine I was in love with her, behaving accordingly. I pushed a finger in and could feel the stalactite of her hymen. I was careful not to break it. At one point, I had a finger either side. She raised her hips, offering the pelvic cup to me. I sipped and drank noisily, satisfied that her wedding night would be the first of many nights of sexual frustration as she tried to communicate her sexual needs to hubbykins without indicating a lack of sexual prowess on his part. It provided an incentive to develop her very own "enviable command of the English language."

Next came Lizzie. She had her own flat. Beautiful hardwood floors and lovely high ceilings. She also had hairs on her arse. That was crime enough, but crime number two? She really liked me.

Soon take care of that.

She was freshly jilted from a long-term relationship and was very delicate. I had two others on the go when we met for our first date. My nervousness made Lizzie more comfortable. She thought it was because I was unsure of her feelings for me.

The truth was less endearing.

I was an alcoholic who needed a drink.

I ended up having sex with her on the kitchen floor in the middle of her making some bullshit vegetarian meal. On the dirty tiles as the pots boiled symbolically overhead. The windows steamed up. Her face looking up at me in disbelief, her chin buried under her pushed-up jumper and bra. Eyes wide. Childlike. After I left her there like that, I never saw her again. Later, she left a message on my machine saying I'd raped her.

Emotionally speaking, maybe I did rape her, but physically she was up for it. No question about it. She was loving it. I could see her already storing away the memories as I fucked her. Her face scanning up and down, recording the images like a flesh-covered camera, close-up of his face, pan down for a wide shot of the action below . . . cut.

Maybe there is a law after all. Of nature. Like gravity. An unwritten axiom that governs our emotional dealings.

What you do comes back to you with twice the force—fuck it, three times the force. We are not punished for our sins, we are punished by them.

From the moment I met Jenny, I knew I was going to hurt her. It was just a matter of where and when. I suppose it was no fault of hers that she even looked a little like Pen. It was that fact that seemed to sanction my actions. After being out all night, I was reluctantly heading in the general direction of what I mockingly referred to as home when I realized I needed more booze. There was never enough of the stuff. I even dreamed about it. One night I was drinking whiskey, and even as it was going down my throat, I was thinking, "I want a drink." Tricky one.

Anyway, one of the main obstacles to getting more booze was lack of money. And money ran out because I couldn't always depend on getting more freelance art direction. I had no rent to speak of, since I was ripping off the local council who paid my rent and electricity. All I had to do was go and sign on the dole once every two weeks.

Parties were a good source, especially parties nearing some sort of end. The amateurs were either passed out on the floor or tucked up at home in their little beds.

The music. The brightly lit window. I didn't have to be Sherlock to figure out there was going to be a fridge full of booze. Everyone brought something to appear generous. Especially if the area was fairly well-to-do, but that was a bit more difficult, because I had to have my wits about me for the inevitably intricate verbal exchanges. I had to resist bursting into flames with the fury I felt towards these fuckers. I hated these people most of all. The ones who had their lives given to them, who in my mind never had to work, who didn't appreciate what they had. As a teenager in Deelford I'd had to pick sugar beets in freezing cold fields, wearing only old socks as gloves. The beet would freeze in the furrows and we'd have to kick each one out of its frozen hard earthen socket before snagging the stalk with beet knives. The term "hard work" is relative.

So I'd press the buzzer and say, "Sorry I'm late."

The door would open and I couldn't help smiling as I took the stairs three at a time. If it wasn't already open, the door soon would be. I never looked like a drunk, I just was a drunk. In I went. Hit the toilet first and either puked up to make room for new booze or just get the lay of the land. Then the fridge. Oh, happy white oblong. A miniature hospital in a bruised world.

The clink of music as it opened. The glow from within. There. A full and as yet unopened bottle of cheap wine with some assorted cans of beer, stragglers from six-packs.

Back to the living room with the wine and after getting it into a pint glass so that I wasn't clutching a bottle that might be recognized by its owner.

And there she was. Sitting all alone. By herself on a couch at four AM, at a party where there were only three people left standing. And I was one of them. Long-legged

26

and elegant and definitely out of place, she reminded me of a *Vogue* photo shoot. Beautiful girl in dingy surroundings. The rich well-read daughter of some English MP slumming it in Camberwell.

Anyway, I vowed to fuck her up as soon as I plonked down beside her. Even in my very comatose state, I knew that asking her to dance, though not being able to get off the couch, was endearing. Dancing with a pint of wine in one hand and a joint in the other was mischievous. Before either of us knew it, we were kissing.

Two weeks later she's throwing beer in my face, and three hours after that, I notice her car parked outside my shitty basement flat. I was drunk and wavering on my bicycle. She was in a Ford something or other. As soon as I turned the corner, the car started up and jolted ferociously forward.

The vehicle resembled a mechanized insect whose legs had been plucked and was being poked awake for new tortures. I laughed loud enough for her to hear through the open window, which emitted cigarette smoke.

I tried to behave as if I were on a horse. She started the engine again and steered it angrily away. Angrily because I could hear gears being shoved around. What had caused this futile display of emotion? Mere words.

Earlier that evening she had asked me how I had enjoyed my weekend.

"Not bad," I said. "Got laid."

27

Stunned, she looked at me with the same inquisitive smile that belonged to the question she had just asked.

Beer hit my face with such force I thought she'd slapped me. But I had not just delivered the line; it had been accompanied by The Smirk. Penelope had felt its girth, and now it was Jenny's turn. I'd never had beer thrown in my face before. It was flattering. Jenny rose, whipped her jacket from the back of her chair, and left. After slowly licking some splashed beer from my lips, I exchanged a look with the barman that said *Chicks!* and returned to my as-yet-untouched beer. Not for long.

Speaking of slap-happiness and the art of The Smirk, it had been a long time since I begged to be beaten up. The Swan in South London was the ideal setting for just such an endeavor.

Very Irish, very fist-happy. Many, many bouncers. They'd stand on stools, the better to police the goings-on, perpetrated by heavily drinking Irish exiles like me. I was deep in conversation with a tall red-haired man from Dublin. There was much jostling for position as the other exiles attempted to get a little closer to their beloved homeland via Guinness.

The spot that the Dub and I occupied was sacred. Right in front of the counter. It was necessary to get there at three in the afternoon to occupy such a position. I'd been there since one. So I turn to the Dub and quite truthfully inform him, "I've been listening to your shit all day and I'm fuckin' sick of it. I wouldn't mind, but to top it all off, you have to be from Dublin."

He immediately head-butted me with such force that I was able to see blood dollop into my pint glass. And I debated whether I should try to strain the blood through my teeth in order to salvage the inch of cider left in the bottom of the glass. I began to see it as important that I contain the dripping blood in the glass. Mustn't for some reason get the place all bloody.

I decided instead to announce, "One of us is going to leave this bar, and it isn't going to be me."

I looked up at my assailant, whose face bore the throes of bloodlust.

Freeze-frame.

I have seen that expression only three times. This was the first. The next was when I was knocked from my bicycle by the "hired" motorcyclist and was waiting for the ambulance people to ascertain whether I had serious injuries.

I was lying on my back, afraid to look down at my legs. On the top floor of a passing double-decker sat an old lady in a brown coat. The bus had to stop, presumably because of the general commotion. The old hag's expression was exactly the same as the one our Dublin friend is wearing now. Look at him. Ginger stubble, tongue slightly protruding from between fleshy lips—a cunt if ever I saw one. Other heads protruded into what might have been my last patch of sky, but it was her face that dominated my wait for the ambulance.

29

Lying there, I was still listening to Elvis Costello's "Accidents Will Happen," I kid you not. My Walkman, although askew, was still on and still playing. That old cow up there looking down from on high seemed to be nodding in time to Mr. Costello's sentiments. I tried to read from the old lady's face how badly I was hurt. I wished I'd known her better, because if she was a complete bitch, the slight smile on her face meant that I was fucked and my legs were mincemeat.

But if she was a nice caring person who fed pigeons and stroked strangers' dogs, I was in good shape because she was smiling on my behalf. I decided she was a bitch and I was fucked.

The third time I saw the expression was when the girl I loved . . . Hang on a minute, that's what this whole bloody thing is about. We'll get to that.

Unfreeze.

The Dubliner looked as if he'd just had sex with me. It had taken me this long to realize I'd been head-butted. There was no pain. Just a dimming of lights. Like someone turning down one of those knobs inside a living room door.

"No. We'll keep it clean. No glasses," he said.

I immediately knew what this meant. He thought I was going to glass him, or the thought to glass me had occurred in him.

I was concentrating my attention on directing the strange dribbling blood, which could well have been coming from the ceiling, into the pint glass in my right hand. For some reason it had become important not to mess up the floor of the Swan.

To be glassed is to receive a pint glass in the face. The mouth of the glass is positioned around the chin and under the nose. A great deal of force is then applied with the ball of the hand to the base of the glass. The handsome face that hovers over the writing of these pages can only wince at the thought of what could have occurred that evening.

So there I was holding a half-pint of my own blood and he wants me in the worst possible way.

Suddenly he was jerked upward as if sucked by a huge vacuum cleaner. Understanding his imminent ejection, the Dubliner reached for the collar of my coat and pulled me along with him. We formed a reluctant conga train, the locomotive for which was two, then three newly unperched bouncers.

Ah yes, nothing like a quiet drink.

Dub wanted to get me outside in order to give me a more leisurely pummeling, but I simply stepped out of the coat and back to my position and a freshly pulled pint of delicious draft cider.

On the house. One of us did leave the bar after all. My coat was brought back folded and presented to me by one of the heroic staff of the Swan. Long may it prosper.

After Penny? There was . . . let's see . . . I still can't remember her name. She was, or claimed to be, a designer. Wild curly brown hair. Shiny. Attractive. Thirty-three, looked

31

thirty-eight. Old when you're twenty-nine. Mind you, I felt eighty.

"You like trees?"

That was all I said to her. She told me later that my question enthralled her. She figured out what I was up to much faster than any of the others. But not in time. I spent an excruciating day with her one Sunday, waiting for night. She cooked dinner. Chicken. And invited her two burly brothers. I found out later this happened every Sunday. At the time I thought it was for my benefit.

I was never a dope smoker. I was a drinker, you understand. But I was broke that day, so I s-s-s-smoked as much of that shit as I could. All it did was increase my already prominent paranoia to international proportions. I thought the brothers were going to butt-fuck me as an after-dinner treat and then beat me to death with their white fists.

I was high. When it finally emerged, the chicken looked like some felled wildebeest too long in the savanna. Jesus, it frightened me. To my high mind, it was still breathing. A vengeful, seething carcass. Mercifully, someone had brought a bottle of red wine. I had to resist lurching across the table and necking it. One glass I had.

And she had the nerve to drop hints about how much I drank. This from a dopehead? Then I had to wait till the whole pathetic brother-sister thing had expended itself before I was allowed to get into her bedroom and eventually her knickers.

The fear and paranoia I'd had to endure that day fueled each pelvic thrust that followed. A dagger widening an existing wound. Merely an action that was required in order to hurt her later.

The next morning, grateful for the absence of a hangover, I left reasonably refreshed. I even grabbed a piece of chicken on the way out. Never saw her again.

Next?

Catherine had just broken up with her live-in boyfriend and had a young daughter. I hoped to excel myself here. She'd had some problems. Emotional problems. Attempted suicide was touched upon. My ears perked up. I heard "Kill me." If I hurt this woman enough, I could nudge her over the edge into suicide. I'd be helping her do what she really wanted, and it'd be a good test of my powers.

It thrilled me to think I could cause a death by proxy. But she proved too strong or too stupid or both or something. From her, though, I learned the technique that would later save my own life.

I hate to be so dramatic, but that, I believe, is how high the stakes were. The pain involved in a premeditated broken heart would easily compare with a case of assault, and yet no court of law would recognize it as a crime. A broken arm heals.

She quickly fell for me, and I was in a hurry to get to the good bit. Once I knew she was in, I began the water torture. I became less available until I banished her to the wintriest regions of my absence. I waited to hear that she had done away with herself, how handsome I imagined myself at her funeral. Or even better to be burying my dick in someone else as she was being buried in the ground.

I can't tell you how insulted I was when she called and cheerily asked how I was. I couldn't believe it. She was supposed to be in a wheelchair. Crippled with grief. Wearing impenetrable dark glasses and clutching a shiny lock of my flaxen mane before cynically abandoning her life.

No.

She continued to call and inquire after my well-being, which only increased my ill-being. It was the way to win, I had to hand it to her. I couldn't quite accept her nonchalance, but there it was. In retrospect, I think she just wanted to show how well she was taking it. Otherwise, why call? Indeed, you may ask, why write it all down? Who cares? Don't we all have brown water like this gushing under our bridges?

No doubt, but there's a dam up ahead.

In my defense, I could talk about how I was abused by a De La Salle Brother when I was nine. How I'd felt the whole row of desks shaking as he played with his star pupil in the back. How I had to put a safety pin through the fly of my short pants to prevent this young Brother's religious fervor. He'd go up the leg instead, and so I begged my mother to let me wear long trousers. I wasn't old enough, she said, and anyway it was summer and Brother Ollie was only being friendly. It wasn't serious abuse.

I mean, I never took it in the arse.

Brother Ollie was later prosecuted for his crime, and in a way, so was I for mine.

And if you like that, here's another.

My father was shaving. It was a cold morning in Deelford. The light was on above the bathroom mirror, so it must have been winter. He looked as if he was scraping off a big cartoon beard. I wanted attention and tried something like "If you don't blah blah can't-remember, I'll never speak to you again." Then slowly, very slowly, he leaned down with great emphasis. The cream-covered face larger and larger as it neared mine. And from under this comical mask came the three little words that meant so much.

"I don't care."

Even now I feel like I should have capitalized them, but that was just the effect they had on me. He said them very quietly. As if he wanted to make sure the message was for me only. Or maybe he was afraid my mother would hear. No fear of that.

A sort of earthquake took place within me. A panicky crumbling. I'll always remember it. That was the moment I knew I'd have to do this thing alone. This thing being life. Doors closed. Like in Westerns when the bad guy walks down the street and all the townsfolk slam their doors one after another into perspective.

My father was someone who until then had been my only friend. My mother didn't even seem to notice I was around, and to my two brothers and sister I was merely an annoyance who needed to be babysat. Da was the only one who had shown me any affection up to then. Maybe as compensation.

I don't want you staining my newly published pages with your salty eye droplets, so I'll get off this topic now. I will say this, though. Seeds were sown.

Maybe this stuff has links to other stuff that happened later. Maybe not. Maybe I was emulating the only relationship I'd ever had by gaining trust and then breaking it abruptly.

Do with it what you will.

I invited Catherine and some of the others to my thirtieth birthday party, to be held in my back garden. The idea was to create a sort of lasagna of pain. All my ex-girlfriends were to gather in one location. My shitty back garden. These separate personalities, unified by the pain I had caused them, would at last understand the devilish mind that now controlled their futures. Something like that.

It was a mess. I was far too drunk to greet anyone. In fact, such sophistication was secondary when all I wanted to do was ladle the contents of the punch bucket into my already bleary-eyed face. At one point, I dispensed with the ladle and drank straight from the bucket. I assume someone hurt someone somewhere that night, because I never heard from any of them again . . . except Catherine, who called only to inquire as to whether I was all right. Jesus.

Let's just lay a blanket over the proceedings. I was annoyed, though. It was like waking up beside a beautiful girl and not being able to remember the sex. By the way, I mention all this because somewhere out there, these girls are getting on with their lives, and I want them to know what happened to me. That even though I'm walking around free in the world, I did get a dose of my own medicine. And it doesn't matter even if they never read these pages. This is just me trying to be honest with myself. Like a 151-page note to self. I'm not looking for sympathy. I'm far more interested in symmetry.

The one who threw the beer in my face called me six months later still sobbing. This was satisfying to me. And Catherine continued to call and ask how I was. Infuriating, but of course I couldn't let her know this, because it would mean she was winning. Maybe you're beginning to see how futile the whole game was. It went on a while longer until I couldn't just keep up the act anymore. I basically lost the plot.

But hang on, I promised I'd tell you about the one time I hit a girl. A long time ago, before all this other stuff, I was in the Mascot Bar in Deelford. I was leaving with a so-called friend, Lenehan. I was drunk, so was he; so was most of Deelford on a Friday night. The bar was crowded and we had to push our way through the throng. Lenehan was ahead of me, cutting a path. An attractive girl turned around and slapped me really hard on the face. Before I knew what was happening, I had punched her.

37

Now, I don't know about the rest of you irreligious fucks, but in Ireland we don't stand for that kind of behavior. I waited outside the pub for the beating I knew I was about to receive. Didn't matter what the extenuating circumstances were.

I'd hit a girl.

The word rippled through the drunken mass, and it wasn't long before five guys, whom I knew quite well, came out, and after much apologizing and wringing of hands, proceeded to punch and kick me.

But there was no passion in it. And they wouldn't stop till blood was drawn, and no blood would bother to show itself to these amateurs.

From my crouching position I tried my best to insult them. My most reliable gibes had no effect until I accused them of having relatives in Britain.

It was over in seconds.

I remember shaking hands with them. One refused because he was still hurt by what I'd said. I allowed my bleeding eyebrow to run its course unwiped, an advertisement that justice had been done. Why had she slapped me in the first place? Lenehan had put his hand under her skirt as he passed behind her, and she assumed I'd done it.

So I went to Alcoholics Anonymous. And slowly I got better. Eight years later, I still go to meetings. I hope I will always go to them. And I stayed away from the dreaded Female for the next five years.

Five and a half, actually. And my career took off. Big-time. I got a job in a renowned advertising agency in London and won awards for the work my creative partner and I did. We were quite famous at one point. My name is still known. I went to my AA meetings in the evenings and worked as hard as I knew how during the day. I suppose I must have been good at it, because I never really found it that hard to come up with ideas.

It was the awful corporate politeness that I found so draining. Little did I know that London's corporate world was virtually anarchic compared to its American counterpart.

After a while, I became disenchanted with my creative partner in London because I felt he wasn't pulling his weight. I believed myself to be the talented one and I was sick of working with him. We'd been staring at each other across a desk now for four years, and I'd resisted diving across and burying my thumbs in his larynx for the last time.

We ended amicably. We really did. He ended up with another partner in the same agency. I was approached by a headhunter to go to a really good agency in the States based in Saint Lacroix. As soon as the headhunter said the company's name, I knew it was the right thing to do. I was due for two weeks holiday in France with some of my AA friends, so I said we'd talk when I got back. She was keen that I call him from France. So I did.

Killallon Fitzpatrick's creative director was visiting London for a few days, doing interviews.

The conversation that started the ball rolling on the events of the following three years took place in the rattling hallway of an old French farmhouse in the Dordogne with dogs barking and the mistral shaking the windows. I had no idea what he looked like, but his voice sounded hilariously American. Like one of my friends had called to take the piss out of me.

The smell of cooking surrounded me, and it must have made me feel more homely than I had a right to, because I pitched myself to this American as the Irish equivalent of Jimmy Stewart, only half his height and talent. It was what he wanted to hear. He virtually fell in love with me.

He apologized for Saint Lacroix, Minnesota, warning me the city was no London or LA. He said Saint Lacroix got "pretty cold" in the winter, but it wasn't as bad as people made off. You could buy a house there next to a lake for next to nothing.

He thought I was the right sort of age for the job. I was thirty-four. There were lots of lovely ladies working in the agency. He felt sure I'd be popular. Pimp. At the time, though, I was ripe for it. Of course I loved London, but I was bored. I'd gotten the awards, I'd succeeded. Time for something new.

I told him I didn't care if it was cold because all I ever did was work anyway. They had heating, didn't they?

I apologized to him for not being a smoker or a drinker, knowing he'd be thrilled, since Americans were nervous about the British creatives' reputation for hard drinking. Didn't go down well in corporate America.

In addition, I informed him that I was at the age where I was thinking about getting married. There followed a long moment of silence, which could only be satisfactorily explained by him punching the air in triumph and straightening his clothes before continuing. He began to talk like someone I'd known for years, dropping all use of the conditional tense in favor of the future.

My future.

The headhunter called on Monday.

"Graham warmed to you quite a bit," she said, then started using words like "visa" and "resign," which I welcomed. This all took place with my copywriter sitting right in front of me. I had taken to sticking my head, complete with phone, out the window to get some privacy.

It wasn't long before I'd resigned and found myself sitting in my London flat, waiting for work permits to be approved. I was to work freelance from the flat until I was official.

But since I needed to vacate the place to let it out I moved into a hotel in Hyde Park. I found myself fifteen minutes away from my own flat with two strangers living in it and the ink not yet dry on a six-month tenancy agreement and me still without any sign of an approved work permit for the United States. This unsettled state was to become the norm for the next five years.

If I'd known what was about to unfold, I would have stopped everything and gone home to live with my mother.

41

But thanks to AA I had also just signed a new lease of life, and I was determined to use it. After all, what was the point in getting sober if I wasn't going to do something with it? And there were the newcomers to think of. A crazy bastard like me heading off to the States for a new career gave the new AA members hope. Or so my sponsor said.

I did find myself at home in Deelford for a few days before flying to the States. My parents were excited for me but sad for themselves. Since I'd stopped drinking, they really did like having me around. I bought them a Dictaphone and convinced them and myself that we'd exchange taped messages across the Atlantic.

Never happened.

My dad had a rather nasty bubbly cough when he was driving me to the railway station. A month into my new job, in my new country, in my new city, in my new house, I got a call from my mother asking the most ridiculous question.

"Are you sitting down?"

I knew immediately that my dad was dead. Only he wasn't. She said he was doing poorly and that I should expect to come back at any moment. My new bosses were very understanding and even helped me book a flight. You get a cheaper flight if you can prove you have a seriously ill relative. You simply give them the hospital phone number. So I flew back, and I still feel guilty about the fact that I hoped my father would die within the week I had allotted for my quality time at home.

Ever the gentleman, he obliged. He was dusted, dead, and buried with a day to spare, and to my shame, I was back at work the Monday after. Well, I was under pressure, wasn't I? I needed to impress my new boss and my old ones in London. I wanted to show them that they'd made a big mistake by not treating me better. Truth is, they hadn't treated me that badly. It just felt convenient to dislike them. The real reason I needed to get away from London was that I hated my creative partner. Obsessively so.

I remember one day standing with one of those big long beveled-edge rulers they use for cutting card with a scalpel. It's basically a blunt sword. He was standing there to my left. Suddenly I felt faint. I didn't fall over or anything. I just checked out for a few seconds. I saw a kind of yellow mist.

When I came back, I was terrified I'd look down and see him lying there with his head smashed in. That was the day I stuck my head out the window and called the headhunters. I was afraid of what I might do if I stayed working with him. And it was better to leave the country than to worry about meeting him in the bitchy streets of London. Or maybe I just needed a change.

Newly arrived in my new country, my new city, I wasn't interested in girls. Not in the least. When I think about the chances I missed, I just want to sob. A foreigner like me in the Midwest really stands out. Mind you, I did ask one gorgeous girl out, but she said she was going steady, so I

43

thought, "Fuck it, if I can't have a beaut, then I'm not play-ing." The other thing was, of course, that I didn't want to get stranded there with two kids and a dog. I knew from the mo-ment I landed that I'd have to get out.

I thought a year would do it. I was wrong. I bought a house, but that was just to convince them I was serious. A house was easy to sell in a buoyant market. And if I played my cards right, I'd make some money on the fucker . . . and anyway, when was I ever going to be able to afford a Victo-rian house with hardwood floors and a cute swing seat on the veranda, like the house in *The Waltons*? The agency talked to the bank to help me get it.

The house was great for about a month.

In the meantime, I was getting to know the insides of air-ports pretty well. In America, taking a flight is like taking a bus in England. You get on a plane for a meeting. Especially if you are based in Saint Lacroix, Minnesota. The first job they put me on was a huge project overseeing the commer-cials for the car company BNV linkup with the Shane Pond movie *Tomorrow Forever Cries*.

Their new model, the 9T, was being featured in the movie, as was their new motorbike, the T2600 Surfer. They wanted three commercials and three print ads to announce this highly attractive association of icons.

It was a pain in the arse. You had to feature the car prom-inently and show clips from the movie. Very difficult task. Very difficult to get a nice clean idea while having to include all those separate elements. Then on top of that, we had to deal with three different clients: BNV North America, BNV Germany, and DGR Pictures. It took nearly nine months and three times as many flights to get the bastard finished.

In my office on the twenty-seventh floor of an ominous gray skyscraper looking out on the flatness of the Midwest, stretching for hundreds of miles in every direction, I might just as well have arrived on the moon.

It reminded me of a sci-fi program on BBC called *Space 1999*. There were a lot of similarities. The interiors of the moon base were all clean lines and high tech, and the views out the windows were barren and stark. The inhabitants of the base were all handpicked, highly civilized, and above all, disciplined. This was a big thing at Killallon Fitzpatrick. The ability to smile while under duress. They loved that. They liked you to suffer quietly.

And I got pretty good at it. I was five years sober. This was what I stopped drinking for. This was the kind of thing I would never have been able to do. I mean, on paper it was great. House. Job. Money. Move to the States. When I was drinking, there was no way I would ever have been offered this kind of situation. And I congratulated myself that I hadn't fallen into the trap of having a girlfriend, because I would never have been able to go if I had. I resolved to resist any advances by any girl from anywhere in the midwestern region. I was no fool. I was not going to let myself get stranded for the rest of my life with some gorgeous wife and blond kids as

45

Killallon Fitzpatrick slowly turned up the heat until I cracked like spring ice.

I got myself hooked up with the local AA groups, which were great. I began to feel better. Saint Lacroix is the capital of rehab. They have more rehab centers than anywhere else in the States. This was one of the reasons I felt so comfortable about moving there in the first place. Less comforting was my discovery that right next door to the biggest of these treatment centers there is a bar. Inside that bar there is a sign. It reads, "AA Chips Exchanged." For every year you stay sober, you receive a little metallic coin called a chip. This bar offers free booze for one night to any lapsed member of AA willing to spend his chip. The wall behind the bar is covered with chips.

As long as I didn't drink and didn't get into a relationship, I'd be able to get back to London and resume life and look back on this whole period as an interesting lapse in concentration. Either way, I was looking out my window after having been flown over and paid quite a bit—I was making $300,000 a year. My ego had been fluffed to the point of ejaculation, my favorite pieces of furniture had been carefully packed and shipped; my mother had been sent a huge bouquet of flowers sympathizing with the loss of her husband, my father. The unspoken, unwritten expectation hung over me: *Okay, big shot, let's go.*

That was pretty freaky, but I didn't mind because I was in a good position. If I fucked up, it didn't really matter; I was in a foreign country. If I did well, it just meant their trust was well placed. And of course I'd make sure the "folks back in London, England" knew all about it.

So I came home to my big Victorian house in the evenings, after my AA meeting, and I liked the fact that I hardly had any furniture. It appealed to me to be living in a house with just a few bits and pieces. The scarcity reminded me of a Deep Purple album cover that featured pictures of a huge country house in France, with recording equipment and wires and cool-looking fuckers strewn everywhere. This was the effect I strove for.

But no one else appreciated the irony of a mostly empty house owned by a shaven-headed Irishman who didn't seem responsible enough to have been given a mortgage. This amused me. It would not have seemed unnatural if someone had kicked in my door one day and said, "There's been a mistake. Get out." I would have left quietly because I really didn't think I deserved such good fortune.

This was linked with feelings of guilt and shame over what I had been doing to people when I was drinking. This need to hurt was lessened when I stopped drinking. Maybe it was replaced with a need to hurt myself.

My neighbors tried to welcome me, but they didn't understand that I could never be seen with them voluntarily. It was okay if someone knocked on my door or invited me over for a beer, which quickly became a Coke. Irony could be achieved under these conditions. All this was fine until I was forced to borrow a lawn mower.

47

American lawns are loaded with social and political meaning. There is a law somewhere that says you have to maintain your lawn or the neighbors can force you to. I knew nothing of this and immediately reveled in the possibility of allowing my front and back gardens to return to nature. A polite knock on my front door changed all that.

The polite knock has a lot to answer for in this world. There he was, frown on forehead, hand on heart, leaflet in hand. The State of Minnesota personified.

"Mornin'."

"Oh, hi," I said, feigning surprise after watching the fat fuck trespass his way to my front door.

"I was noticin' how you were havin' some trouble with your lawn care, and well, I think you might find this leaflet interestin'."

The lazy pronunciation of words like "interesting" is code for informality. Saying *interest-in* instead of *interest-ing* is their way of announcin' they are just regular guys.

"Oh, thank you very much, that's really very kind of you," I said, drawing on the ten years of Britishness that lay in reserve for moments like these.

Very humbling, though.

The lawn mower I borrowed from yet another neighbor had a full tank of gas, and even I knew that it would need to be returned full. Such a task would entail a conversation with a gas station attendant.

"You're not from around here, are ya?"

Every time.

I'd change my accent. Flatten it a little. I could pretend I was from New York or Los Angeles. At least they wouldn't feel as if they'd landed such a catch.

If you said you were Irish but from London, it was as if one had performed a method of fellatio so bizarre that their eyes would glaze over and a little happy smile would bend the momentarily speechless mouth.

Then the thanking would start. I represented every post-card, movie, or rumor that had ever emanated from Europe. And everybody knows ambassadors need to be diplomatic. I'd just pick up whatever I'd been trying to buy and leave. I hated them. Forgive me, but I fucking hated them. When I got back to Ireland for a break at Christmas, I couldn't even look at a McDonald's sign without wanting to spit. I'm all right now because I live in New York. Thank you, God, for New York.

But the Midwest is something else.

My boss used to point at girls who had just joined the agency and whisper, "She's single." I couldn't believe it. He actively encouraged me to go out with girls who worked for the agency. The theory being, of course, that if I married within the company, then the company would live forever. And then I might even have kids.

Or he'd say, "You come in on the bus, don't you?"

"That's right."

"I met my wife on the bus."

49

For fuck's sake.

He was a decent enough sort of guy. I don't think he did it cynically. He just seemed to have bought the whole package. Advertising is false. Once you know that, you've got a chance. But he believed the hype. The wife/the house/the kids/the dog. I think he was good at what he did and a great boss; he just didn't have enough suspicion.

I am of course aware that reading this, you could conclude that any unhappiness I experienced was homemade. That my suspicion of my boss's good intentions was in itself the problem. But it's what I do. I suspect. It's the other stuff I find hard. Like trusting people. Foreign concept. Just ask any of the billions of girls I haven't dated.

So the boss had his motives and I had mine. I just wanted to get Killallon Fitzpatrick on my résumé for one year. That was it. A year. I was panicking after three months. If I hadn't just moved into the house, I'd have left right then and there. So I suppose it worked out for the best.

Anyway, it took almost two years before I got out, but that's not what I want to talk about. I mention all that stuff about advertising only to give you a background against which to project the rest of my story. The real point is to tell you how I purged myself of my sins against women, and indeed, against myself. They say you're not punished for your sins, you're punished by them.

Also, I'm completely paranoid. I mean, seriously paranoid. Not just mildly interested in the fact that there may be people who don't necessarily have my best interests at heart. No. The word is "paranoid." Another word is "self-centered." I don't like that one as much, though. Doesn't sound medical enough.

The paranoia is worth mentioning because it sometimes fuels my crazy thinking. Like the time I thought Pen was paying people to follow me. Why she was doing this was not totally clear. My paranoia gives me only broad scenarios. It's too lazy to go into details. I believed that people, ordinary people on the street, were operatives in her employ. Their mission was to disrupt me psychologically. Every time I left my basement flat in Camberwell, an old lady or a man with his daughter became enemies I had to avoid.

I would wear an expression that in my poor confused mind exuded the following statement: "I know who you all are. I'm going to give you the impression that I don't know just so we can keep this charade going, but in truth I know. So don't push it."

You may wonder what this expression might look like. I'll tell you. Cocky anger. A snarl with a slight smile—imperceptible, but there. I know you know I know recurring to infinity. Of course, the fact that I've told you all of the above does slightly dent my credibility concerning the below, but my only obligation here is to relate what happened.

This is my therapy. I'm too fucked up to go and see a therapist, and to be honest, I wouldn't trust him anyway, would I? I mean, it's not as if my paranoia is going to clock off for an hour a week. And I've got enough on my plate, having to be a genius during the day and an AA leading light at night. I heard someone say somewhere that it's possible to write the sickness out of yourself. And who knows, maybe someone will benefit.

Anyway as I said, I live in New York now. I am much happier, and even though the way I got here wasn't exactly graceful, I love it here now. It is amazing to me that I do. The first two months I spent in Manhattan were the nearest I ever got to suicide. It was funny how it came to me. The thought of killing myself.

It'd been only a week since Aisling rejected me in Georgina's, and somehow during that period I was able to do a decent impersonation of myself. You'd think it would have been easier considering I'd been my own understudy for years.

Taking breaks to go outside and cry helped.

So I found myself looking out the window on the fifteenth floor of the New York branch of the same agency I worked for in Saint Lacroix. It was around the end of March and very humid. Nothing like as bad as it gets in July, but humid nonetheless, and much worse, because they don't turn on the air-conditioning until the summer.

So there I was, gasping for air—a waft, a ripple of merciful breeze—when I looked down on the cement below. It was the back of the building, so I was looking down on those weird fans they always have in New York. Fuck knows what they are. But there was a little rectangular clearing of combed concrete in the center. Gently it came to me. Gently, now. Not like some crazed jump cut that makes you blink.

Calmly I saw myself lying as if in REM sleep, perfectly framed in that rectangular area. Left leg bent, right leg straight, left arm bent with the palm of the left hand down. Right arm straight down by my side. My head turned sideways on my left hand, as though asleep on a pillow. Just above my head, and under my left hand, there appeared to be a very neatly arranged abstract area of red. Like a big flattened flower upon which my head rested. Rested. I looked peaceful. Beyond pain.

I was in a lot of pain, you see. But it had been caused by an abstract blade. What I mean is, the pain was physical, the cause wasn't. I suppose some people would say I was suffering from a broken heart. Or you might say it's just life. Or maybe it's alcoholism minus the alcohol. After all, I'm five years sober at this point.

True, but something else was going on. How do I know? I don't. I just can't believe that my emotional state could be explained by such an adolescent term as "broken heart." I'm willing to be wrong, but I don't know how anyone will ever be able to prove it, so I'm safe enough. That's another thing you'll learn about me as we go on. I don't like to take risks. I'll offer you the possibility that I'm wrong only if I'm fairly sure I'm right.

Makes me appear more humble.

For example, if I believe something I've thought of is funny, I'll pretend that someone else said it in order to get an unbiased reaction from the person I'm telling it to. If that person laughs, I congratulate myself on having come up with something funny, truly funny, because it achieved laughter from my acquaintance without feeling I'd be hurt if he hadn't found it funny.

Where was I? Suicide. Yes, suicide comes like an old friend. I had just moved from Minnesota to be with the girl I loved but that girl didn't exist. I couldn't find her anywhere. I could see her anytime I wanted. I could talk to her day or night. She was very happy to be my friend. The ultimate demotion. The word "friend" registered as *eunuch* in my fevered mind. I could see her, but only as a non-man.

Exquisite torture.

And it was so hot.

I had so much scary work to do. People to impress. Apartments to see, ideas to generate. I had a strong sense that the world and its inhabitants were trying not to burst out laughing in my face. That they would do that later when I wasn't looking. The thought came to me: "You could use a rest." I felt myself nod at this. And then it'd all be over. No more pain. Cool air on the way down.

It made sense. Especially the cool air on the way down. That was very attractive. Something stepped in and said no. I suppose I was kind of numb for a month or so after that, but that picture of myself framed on a gray mattress will stay with me forever. My paranoid Polaroid. That's one picture she definitely had a hand in.

So, let's see, we've gone too far, let's reverse a little. Right, I'm in Saint Lacroix, and it's around August. My dad has died and now lives in the ground outside Deelford in the corner of a churchyard near his own dad. Strange to think of that. I was alive and well and waiting for what everyone was waiting for in Saint Lacroix. The winter. If you're smiling and brimming with fun and full of lip, some Lutheran type will savor the moment before saying, "You wait."

They don't like happiness.

Seriously. All that Swedish/Norwegian influence has the same effect as a big wet hairy blanket that freezes hard in the winter for at least six months. Fucking freezing. If you live there, the frozenness becomes relative.

I felt a sense of elation if I woke up one morning and the asshole on the TV told me it was minus seventeen degrees instead of the minus thirty it was the day before. I was ready to break out my shorts and sandals. To any sane person, from the real world, it's still fucking freezing. Never before has the picture of a girl in a bikini brought forth such feelings of incomprehension in me. There, in an ad for holidays on the side of a bus stalled in a snowdrift. Smiling and tanned, resting her head on one hand, she says, "You are a fucking idiot." As the bus crept past me, her lips actually seemed to move as she inquired, "Why are you freezing your balls off in semi-Siberia?"

55

I would have cried, but my tears would probably freeze and blind me. I didn't know what tears did at these temperatures. How could I? I wasn't from here. I had no experience of this. I trained myself to derive a perverse pleasure from the surrealism of the place. Hell in reverse. Instead of fire and brimstone, it was snow and ice.

There exists in Minnesotan myth a fabled phenomenon: At certain temperatures—somewhere in the minus forties—a cup of coffee can be thrown in the air and it will crystallize before hitting the ground. I heard this at least three times before experiencing my first winter.

The purpose, I suppose, of this little fact was to scare the fucking shit out of newcomers. It has a beautiful disguise built into it in the sense that on the surface it appears to be an interesting fact worthy of mentioning.

It even has what we call in advertising a mnemonic. That is to say, it has one memorable thing that you can bring away from it. The story would come under the heading of "The One Where Coffee Freezes in the Air." It has that fact as a decoy for the storyteller. The storyteller can impart his tale in the guise of one who is merely sharing knowledge. The truth, though, has more to do with the satisfaction wrought from the face of the listener as he realizes just how fucking freezing it must be for a cup of coffee to turn into crystals in midair.

Then he has to decide whether to react honestly (blanch and throw up) or dishonestly (feign interest in the actual physics). One particular night, my Victorian house had a bed, a table, a hi-fi, and a Texas friend in it. I mention what state he's from only because it removes any authority you might attribute to him concerning his knowledge of all things fucking freezing.

"Dude, it's minus thirty-five outside. Let's try that coffee deal."

"It's not cold enough," I said, fearful of having to make coffee and demonstrate my ignorance of the coffeemaker, which I had never used and only had because someone gave it to me as a moving-in present.

"Dude, with wind chill it's plenty cold."

"Well, I don't want to make coffee. I don't think I have any."

"Dude, water'll do fine. Boil some water."

What the hell, I was bored listening to how great Texas was anyway. I had some saucepans, believe it or not, and before you could say "Remember the Alamo!" we had a saucepan of water on the boil.

"Dude, wait till it's bubblin'. It's gotta be bubblin'. Otherwise it won't work."

And bubble it did. The kitchen opened onto the back garden, and there were a couple of steps down to it. I opened the mosquito door, which I had learned to keep shut at all times, even in the winter. You can't take chances with those little bastards. Then after stepping into my carefully shopped-for goose-down all-in-one duvet-cum-flak jacket (for all intents and purposes a flexible shed), I opened the kitchen door an eye's width. Tex-Ass was having none of it. In just a T-shirt, he grabbed the saucepan handle with both hands and, careful not to spill anything, motioned the steaming pot toward the night. I pushed the door open wide and flicked on the outdoor light.

Well, fuck it, if it was true, I didn't want to miss it. So out he went to the top step. It looked like there was smoke coming out of the saucepan now because of the contrast between hot and cold. He had the pan in both hands in front of him. He said "Dude" one more time just because there was an opportunity to, and leaning back, he flung the contents into the black sky. There was a little glint among all the steam and then an almighty roar.

He looked directly ahead and shuddered. At first I thought he was cold, but then I realized it was the other way around. The boiling water had gone up and then down, landing on him. Far from crystallizing, the water only cooled slightly, and this fact alone saved him a trip to the hospital.

Funny how quiet it gets when there's four feet of snow on everything. How surreal to step out of my house of a morning and find myself on the set of *Doctor Zhivago*. The hairs in my nostrils went hard, and if I tried to pick my nose, they would break. The air hurt my lungs. I could feel the weight of it in my chest. I may have had a big funny hat on, but I had better have those ears covered.

Extremities were the first to go. Ears, fingers, toes.

That's what you always hear about Captain Scott types having their toes bitten off. You need those funny hats with the flaps. Oh, yes. The winter doesn't just degrade your physical sensibilities; it assaults your sense of taste with equal fervor. But the purifying effect of cold, sterile air was somehow comforting. It allowed a conspiratorial sloth to envelop the soul. Conspiratorial, because others would assist you in the postponement of life. For that is what it was. I said to myself, "Well, nothing can be achieved in this. The weather is so inhospitable, there's no point in starting a new project till the weather improves." Which I ended up hoping would be never.

You'd be in the right place with such hopes. People got so fat in Minnesota winters they couldn't go out, which in turn contributed to their getting even fatter. They had constant supplies of food delivered to their door. The snowplows were keeping the roads open only to feed these fat fucks pizza. The snowplow drivers were not exactly svelte themselves. But you know what, I'm trying to stop saying that. They said that a lot in Minnesota. "You know what this" and "you know what that." To me, "you know what" should be reserved for something truly surprising.

"You know what?"

"What?"

"Fuck you."

Anyway, I was going to say before I interrupted myself that I'd been prepared for the winter so much by every person I met that when it descended, it wasn't that bad. I was told I had two of the mildest winters in a very long time. I didn't mind, I didn't feel cheated. I can still say, hand on heart, that I weathered two Fucking Freezing Minnesota Winters.

I served my time.

Combine my celibacy with my Arctic experiment and you've got a potent cocktail of pent-up aggression and self-denial. I began to understand those who felt the urge to walk into McDonald's with an Uzi, demanding satisfaction. Admittedly, if I had ever entered such an establishment with that kind of mayhem in mind, I'd be the kind of guy who'd refuse to turn the gun on himself. Much better to shoot yourself in the leg and pretend to be one of the victimized. That way you got to see the aftermath on TV from a hospital bed. But wouldn't the other victims identify you? Not if you'd been careful enough to cover your face, they wouldn't. Okay, okay, so I've thought about it.

One year in Minnesota felt like three. I owned a Victorian house in one of the best neighborhoods in Saint Lacroix. By this time I'm making $300,000 a year, my mortgage has risen to $4,500 a month, and I'm stressed out of mind. My salary gave me about twice what I needed to pay the monthly mortgage, so I could afford it, but even so, I'm not rich.

I thought I'd be rich. I anticipated being nonchalant about money. Having expensive toys like jukeboxes and sound systems and pool tables and bubble-wrapped antiques.

No. But hang on, I was going to make a fortune when I sold the house, wasn't I? Yes, of course I was. Now get back to work.

I was convinced that every $4,500 I gave to this Victorian was like putting money in the bank. No. Suitably enough, considering the temperature outside, all I succeeded in doing was freezing the loan in its tracks. Nothing was being paid off. Except the interest and the insurance.

Basically I was only paying the rent on the loan. And of course I didn't make anything like a fortune on that whore of a house when I eventually did sell it. I sort of almost after tax rebates broke kind of even. Barely. So in retrospect it didn't hurt as much as it might have. But at the time I had a house tied around my neck, a determination not to touch anything that might lead to contact with a female of any species, let alone human, and a desire to get back to London so strong I could taste it in the air around me.

I waited for *The Observer* like a wino waiting for opening time. My sadness when the magazine was sold out or just didn't arrive because of—wait for it—freezing weather was incommunicable. And when it was in, I'd clutch it to my chest. It was already three days old, but so what?

I loved the clever, laid-back, almost bored-with-themselves way the writers put across their points. I never realized just how urban I really was. Moving from London to Saint Lacroix was more of a shock than moving back to Ireland would have been. I found that out soon enough

61

when I spent a few nights in New Dublin. It was so vibrant and young on that Christmas Eve, I had to hold back tears because I knew I would soon have to go back to Minnesota.

The Observer, Time Out London—in fact anything from London—I loved those publications. Typical home-sick behavior, I suppose, but I tip my imaginary hat to *The Observer*, especially for its part in saving the patrons of McDonald's and other Minnesota eateries from a messy end. Also films. French films. Yes, I had a DVD player. I don't anymore. All I have to do these days is take a leisurely stroll up Avenue A and I've got all the entertainment I need.

But back then it was like droplets of moisture on the cracked lips of the dehydrated to see a French film. Not just because the French, God bless them, make great films, but to see those old streets and buildings and that weather all damp and moist—Jesus Christ, I loved looking at that. I even took photographs of paused scenes at certain points. This was during my second year in Minnesota, when I had really begun to lose it. I still have the photos somewhere. I needed to keep connected with Europe any way I could.

My biggest fear was that I would end up accommodating expressions like "You betcha" and "You're darn tootin' " into my vocabulary. So with my French films (Claude Lelouch was my favorite director), my English newspapers, and my Irish self, I kept the European flag flying in the ferocious Minnesota gales.

Two years. Two years physically, but spiritually it felt

like eight. I trudged to the bus stop every morning through the new snow and crunched my way home in the evenings. Sometimes I'd walk around the lake, which was only a hundred yards from my frosted front door. Sounds nice, doesn't it?

Steady.

One of the most telling symptoms of hypothermia, against which one must be constantly vigilant, is hallucinations. The imaginary attraction of what was before you. I'd tell myself, "You've got a great job, a great house. The people are really nice. The girls are gorgeous," etc. I should have loved it. You'd have thought a thirty-four-year-old unmarried man heading out there and finding himself surrounded by such conditions would be thanking his lucky stars. But I was cursing myself for having created these circumstances. If it had been happening to someone else, I would have approved and even wished him well, but because it was happening to me I couldn't bear it, it was as if I had been miscast in my own life. If I saw someone across the street who did the things to me that I routinely do to me, I'd run in the opposite direction. But I can't, can I?

I'm married to me.

And from what I could see, marriage to other people was the norm out there. I didn't drink or smoke and I was fairly well behaved. At least outwardly. I should have been the perfect candidate for some self-respecting clean-gened Minnesotan girl. But fuck it, the big toothy smiles, the thick needy niceness. That crazy wide-eyed stare. I still don't know what that was. Zoloft? Stupidity? In New York, everyone just looked hurt. It seemed more honest. Maybe I just identified with them.

So I decided I'd had enough of this. I'm gone. This before my first year was over. I picked a real estate agent from one of my AA meetings, since I didn't trust the people who sold the house to me. I truly believed my former real estate agents would pick up the phone and call the company I worked for and tell them I wanted to sell my house. They had invested a lot in getting me to Minnesota, after all, and might be interested to hear why I wanted to leave after only twelve months in their employ.

I offer this statement in defense of my paranoia. It wasn't until I actually physically tried to leave that I found out how hard it was going to be. The house did not receive one offer. Over that whole summer nobody made me an offer of any kind. I can't tell you how terrified I became with every passing day, the summer ticking away, the winter approaching, and the possibility of another year in exile. Nothing sells in the winter.

Sleepless, I would sit bolt upright in the bed. I'd curse the walls that surrounded me, and yes, I would cry. Big gasping, self-pitying sessions of sadness. I don't think anyone ever saw me (at least I hope not), but sometimes I would end up on my hands and knees. It was the only position where I could breathe. Sometimes I'd end up laughing from relief.

The job was very demanding, too, so I don't suppose that helped. In fact, work was a lot of the problem. Knowing I wasn't going anywhere with that house tied around my neck, they gently applied more and more pressure. It would take at least a couple of months to sell a house. Therefore they were comfortable giving me some of their toughest accounts. I wasn't going to resign in the middle of anything. Or if I was, they'd get plenty of warning. The more the pressure built, the more I wanted to sell the house.

But the fucker didn't budge, and I even started to lower the price on my real estate agent's advice. I wasn't too fond of him by the time we were finished. Coming home to what was a very cute house and cursing him and it, but mostly myself, for buying it. His advice to me was to dress it. In effect, give the impression someone lived there. Someone normal. So I borrowed furniture, the kind of stuff that would make it look like a middle-aged woman lived there. I tended the garden. Installed flowers for every open house. Mowed the lawns. Became the very thing I relished not being in order to sell that whore of a house.

But it wouldn't budge.

One night I returned home after refusing to go to the company Christmas party. Somehow they had arranged to have two ice sculptures placed on either side of the path to my door. Big cylinders of ice with candles inside.

Quite nice, really.

I kicked them both in. To me, these homely sculptures

represented the fact that I wasn't safe from their prying eyes, even in my overpriced fucking house. I was in a bad way. So I'd come into work and do the best I could. I did good work. But nothing I conceived ever got through. I couldn't help thinking that all they really wanted was to mine ideas and lob them into a communal conceptual pool from which the lifers could draw.

Lifers were their favorites. The ones who would never leave and so were never expected to come up with their own ideas. Loyalty rewarded with stresslessness. They were usually married with kids and a house and so weren't going anywhere. They constantly needed new flesh to feed on. And they got it. Fair enough, once you knew the rules. Pretty scary if you bought the party line, which stated, "We love all of our people. You are part of our family."

Made me want to go and wash. My whole raison d'être was not to become a lifer. Have you ever seen a movie called *The Firm*? That's what it was like. A company that knew your every move and controlled you. Everything was fine until you went against their teachings.

By the way, I fully accept that a lot of what I'm saying is paranoia. All of this and everything that follows could well be my own imaginings and totally unfounded. I mean, the actual facts and figures are true. Dates, salaries, locations, awards, etc. But the motivations and emotions and even the existence of some of the people surrounding those solids are smoke.

I was working for a very weird but brilliant company. I didn't care, because it was interesting to be in the States even if it was only Minnesota and it was beneficial to me because Killallon Fitzpatrick had a reputation for producing fantastic award-winning work. Even if I didn't get anything produced, it was more exciting than sitting in London doing the same stuff I'd been doing for years. I won't pretend I enjoyed it at the time, but now that I'm sitting here in the East Village, extricating myself from London and moving to the States was a great thing to have done.

Anyway, well into my second year there, my fourth year off the booze, I was still refusing to get involved with any female. My favorite masturbation technique was to take a nice hot bath, soap up my baldy lad well and truly, and then give him a good old beating. At one stage I was going to write a screenplay all about my right hand, a love story. There would have been scenes where I let my hand brush against my thigh as a precursor to hitting on mysef. I'd blush. In another, my right hand would get jealous of my left.

Many's the evening I rushed home to make passionate love to myself. Storing away the beautiful asses of the secretaries during the day, I'd mentally combine them into one composite perfectitude of buttockness. It worked. As you can see from the previous pages, it didn't have any perverse effect on my mental or spiritual state. If anything, another room full of McDonald's patrons was spared the inconvenience of drawing on their medical insurance.

Also, I was saved the heartache of having to spend fourteen years married to some woman of Swedish extraction who would need to be paid by my company to marry me in the first place. Imagine all those ice sculptures on my driveway every Christmas (I'm shuddering here and it's August).

Suffice it to say, much masturbation took place during this Minnesotan period. You know, anyone reading this, you would be forgiven for thinking, "What's wrong with this guy? What's his problem? He lands a cool job in the States and all he's done since the beginning of this is whine." Let me just say this, I'm whining in retrospect. At the time I never whined. Not once. I was the picture of humility and gratitude.

"Oh, thank you. Oh no, thank you. Come in on the weekend? Of course, I'm not doing anything anyway. I don't even have a girlfriend, so there's no danger of anything like that getting in the way of your requirements. You don't like that concept? 'Course you don't, it's weak. I should have known better than to present it to you."

I'd all but reverse out of the room bowing. I had to. I was in no position to bargain. With a $4,500-a-month mortgage and no green card, I needed not to piss anyone off. Jesus, as I look back on it, it's even more scary than I let myself realize. Funny that, when things are dodgy and I don't like the way they're going, I move into just-for-today mode. It's an old AA trick for staying off booze. I don't have to do whatever it is forever, I just do it today. It makes even the heaviest shit bearable. But then later when I look back and see just how heavy it was, I exhale.

But hang on, I have to tell you about something that happened the first Christmas after Da died. Remember now, I've been in Minnesota only four months and I won't meet Aisling till the following November. My mother and I were sitting in the kitchen sizing each other up. We were both in shock—her from the fact that her husband of forty years was suddenly missing (she told me she had a dream where they were on holiday and she couldn't find him) and me from losing my father and being uprooted to live in the Arctic.

A roasted turkey with no legs was steaming in the space between us. It was the first time my mother had bought a turkey on her own, and it had seemed like a bargain to her to buy the one that had no legs. It was considerably cheaper than the able-bodied version. After all, she had spent a lifetime having a man to deal with all financial matters, so now the cost of living had become urgent. The turkey steam softened our image of each other that Christmas.

Later during that visit I was doing the chair at the local AA meeting in Deelford. Doing the chair meant a member told his story. How he drank, how he stopped, and what it's like now. At smaller meetings they got tired of hearing the same people again and again, so when someone came home on holiday they were often asked to speak. It was my turn that Sunday. Amongst the regular attendees, many of whom I'd gotten to know quite well over the years, was a very young, well-dressed, blond-haired girl, slender, tall, elegant. Definitely stood out. Could have been a model.

Probably was.

I tried not to embellish my story too much for her sake. I began telling the assorted morning circle about how I used to enjoy hurting people, girls in particular. I touched on the pleasure I got from it, the pleasure I felt when they reacted with such abhorrence. The need I had to hurt. Not unlike some of the stuff I've shared with your good selves, but in a more general way.

I went on to say how I now believed this behavior was linked to my alcoholism, and that I didn't feel the need to do it anymore, and that I still felt like I owed amends to every one of those girls, but that the AA way was not to go back to places where we might cause even more pain. The best amends I could make was to stay out of their lives. I had no right to go back and make their load heavier just to relieve mine.

After I finished my talk, the blond-haired girl came up and thanked me. Standard procedure. But she said some things that didn't sink in until a year, and much turbulence, later. She said she had a friend who liked to do what I'd been talking about. Only she did it to men. The kinds of things I described were very similar to the kind of thing her friend got up to. She said this friend lived in New York now but was originally from Dublin. A photographer's assistant. And if I ever met her, I should be very careful. I must have had my polite face on because she suddenly said, "She knows about you."

This girl was obviously out of her tree. It happened a lot in AA: Someone came in for one meeting and you never saw him or her again. I hoped this would be the case here.

She went on to say she was staying with this so-called scary girl's step-dad that weekend in Deelford and that she'd needed an AA meeting because she couldn't handle the all-night parties. She feared for her sobriety. I immediately imagined satanic orgies going on in that guy's house and was even ready to hear some details until she mentioned his name.

Tom Bannister.

I knew the name very well because he had been my father's solicitor. In fact, when my father died he had been so supportive and helpful that I asked him to keep an eye on my London flat. She had my attention now, but the significance didn't register. Because there was nothing to react to.

Later, much later, I remembered that nine months before this encounter, when I was still working in London, an article had appeared in the *Deelford Gazette* supplied and written by me announcing my appointment as senior art director at Killallon Fitzpatrick. It was the kind of thing local papers loved. Deelford boy does well. I did it as much for my dad as anyone.

He loved to brag to his friends about me.

He even got a mention as the parent of the wunderkind

along with the school I attended and my hobbies (I put writing and music), and I couldn't help but include the fact that I was single. Well, why not? There might be a nice Irish girl out there reading it.

Apparently not.

Could Aisling have read this article during one of her visits? It would explain how she knew about me. "She's evil," said the blonde. She herself had apparently witnessed the awful effect this girl could have on guys. She looked at me for far too long. Like I wasn't taking her seriously enough. I wasn't.

I thought she was just a rich Dún Laoghaire type who'd overdone the coke and was in AA to keep her rich husband happy. Now I think she was trying to warn me. She took on an even more serious tone as she turned to me before leaving. "It's her eyes, that's what does it. They can't believe she could be so bad." I remember thinking it's a pity she's so fucked up because she's very tasty. But I could see that whoever she was talking about had certainly put the fear of God into her. So I thought no more about it. Why would I? There are a lot of people, some of them strange, some of them not, who passed through AA all the time.

I never saw the blonde again. So off I go with a heavy heart back to the tundra that January. I made a pledge to myself that I would leave before the year was out. It was the second time I'd made this promise. It would take slightly longer. I was working on BNV. I was working on BNV only.

It's tough when you are working on only one subject; you can't get any fresh air, so to speak. It's very tough when you're on it for almost two years. Also, it's very draining.

At one point I would resist even making a joke with my small circle of AA friends, because I feared the waste of creative energy would usurp my bank and I'd be depleted when BNV came to make yet another withdrawal. Oh, yes. When you've been on it four weekends in a row, and there's no sunshine or vacation in sight, and you don't want to be in the country, let alone the office, it's important to refrain from spending your reserves.

You may still have a long way to go. And although I promised myself I'd be out soon, my cautious side reminded me that I had said that before. It was now February. Three, maybe four more months of frightening weather still to go. A combination of hiding behind the big broad sheets of *The Observer* and the warm glow of the TV screen, I somehow made it to spring, which lasted about a week, and then the summer was upon us and everything transformed. Where once there was a white sheet of paper there now began to appear the most delicate crayon flicks of grass and leaves and bud and flower.

And the girls.

Unbelievable Aryan examples of breast and thigh. Healthy to the point of insulting. Like well-trained troops circumnavigating the lakes on bikes, Rollerblades, and of course, on foot. The Sexual Infantry. I very quickly learned they were married or about to be. Snapped up early by canny investors. Go ahead, leer. They'd scratch their noses or adjust their various straps, sending me a clear Morse message with the glinting rings.

N-O--C-H-A-N-C-E--P-E-R-V-E-R-T.

Fair enough. The more beautiful and clear-skinned, the bigger and more blinding the glint. It was their fiancé's voice warning me by proxy. Saving me time. How very Minnesotan. Polite. There also seemed to be a great deal of pride in the bulbous nature of a pregnant belly, a phenomenon I had not yet encountered. In London, pregnancy was associated with failure and social death. Here it was encouraged. People got promoted after having a kid. A little fleshy anchor prevented the minds of America's corporate soldiers from drifting too far from its assignments.

Not the place for single males.

Especially single males from somewhere else. Summer in Saint Lacroix is as hot as the winter is cold. Humidity makes the very air thick to breathe. All bared flesh becomes prey to the mighty mosquito, Minnesota's State Bird.

My first summer was worse than my first winter. At least I had been forewarned about the winter. I had to make my own decisions about summer months. Also, Victorian houses don't usually have that coveted air-conditioning installed. It wasn't even invented until the 1960s or 1970s. How's that for an accurately researched fact?

It is my humble opinion that a lot of the civil rights

protests—and indeed, a good portion of this fine country's problems, including the Civil War and the assassination of more than one president—can be attributed to the absence of air-conditioning.

You innocently open your windows in the hope that a breath of a wisp of a breeze of a wind will exhale itself into the airlessness that has become your life. Instead you are prey to a procession of winged and world-weary insectoids trained in the art of psychological warfare.

During the summer, these gaping mouths of Hades disguised as windows belched torture unheard of into my tepid home. I sought refuge in a bath full of cool water, but I needed to stay submerged for as long as lungs allowed. I could still be bitten on the face.

I learned.

Early evening was when I was at my most succulent to the winged carnivores. There are ten thousand lakes in Minnesota. That's a lot of humidity when it gets hot. Humidity means mosquitoes. There's a story going around. An elderly couple went camping. They'd been warned of the locust-like mosquito presence. They pitched their tent. They smeared themselves in what they believed to be mosquito repellent.

They were both found dead. A can of mosquito attractant lay empty between the two corpses. The product was designed to be left outside the tent, thereby attracting the "pesky critters" away from your sleeping body. According to the story, the husband woke up covered in bites and said to his equally be-cratered wife, "Just imagine how bad it would be if we hadn't put on the cream, honey."

No, I don't believe it either. But the summer had its moments. Eleena was one of those girls with a caricature version of what a girl's body should look like. She was also a member of Saint Lacroix AA and therefore more than qualified to attend the Saint Lacroix annual barbecue. She was tanning herself on a little collapsible sun bed when her mobile phone roused her.

Flicking it open, she squeezed out the following words in a voice at least three times higher than her IQ, "Hi, Jimmy, I'm just lying here toasting my buns. Wanna come flip me over?"

She looked like Sophia Loren juxtaposed on a Minnesotan lawn. It was difficult not to attribute the sizzle from the nearby grill to her. Later that day, I masturbated furiously over this image in the coolness of my own bath. Oh yes I did.

Summer, though, is not what we're here to talk about. Come September, things cooled down a little bit. It was the nicest time of the year. The leaves went all amber and the air got fresh and there was even the odd breeze. Oh, happy day. Along with it came yet another BNV assignment. I was sick of working on the account. The very sight of one on the street (I've never owned a car) made me wince. Still does. But that didn't matter, they'd spent all their money bringing me over to this fine country and they wanted me working on BNFUCKINV.

With no offers on the house, I had no leverage, so I bit my already scarred tongue and mumbled something about this being the last time I was ever going to work on this silly car account. They knew and I knew they were just nodding at me out of boredom. With a copywriter, I set to work on the project, and pretty soon we had something not half bad.

Next, we needed a photographer. I took a notion, or the notion was gently introduced to me by clever account executives, that a still-life photographer called Brian Tomkinsin would be an interesting change. Still-life guys normally shot knives and forks and shoes and shit. Never or rarely cars. This of course made BNV nervous, but not for long. I did a sell on them with my Irish/English accent, and soon I was on a plane to New York with a whole week of shooting ahead of me. This is my favorite part about working in advertising.

The shoots are superb. Even the print shoots. You got a cool hotel, you got everything expensed, you get a week away, maybe more, from Minnesota, you got a half-decent shot for your book (portfolio), you got some time off from working on new concepts with which to feed the furnace. You got a breather.

All I knew about New York was what I'd gleaned five or six years before during Saint Patrick's week. Basically, I was out of my fucking mind the whole time I was there, and it struck me as a miserable, dark and dangerous place. This, however, was not the New York that greeted me now.

'Twas October, and autumn was having its way in what

I soon learned was SoHo. Beautiful to the eye, comely to the touch, mesmerizing in abundance. To the starved eyes of one such as I, there seemed to be an excess of muchness. Colors, smells, textures, nationalities—you've heard all of this before. The studio was, still is, on Broadway right on the lip of SoHo and the brow of the East Village and the cusp of Nolita. I can remember being afraid to look, lest I increase the inevitable sadness of having to leave.

I shopped. An unheard-of luxury for me. Oh, they had shops in Minnesota, but in New York no one asked where you were from. They just didn't give a fuck.

God, I loved that.

The shoot went well, and though I wasn't thrilled about the hotel they put me in, the Tannery on 35th and Madison (not very nice), I was enjoying the porn channels. Why not, it was on expenses. And my hotel was changed after the first three days. So anyway, the initial shots of the car were done in a different part of town housing a bigger "stoodio." I still couldn't tell you where that was—not too far away from Broadway, is all I can remember. So the next stage of comping needed to be done from Tomkinsin's Broadway headquarters.

Suited me. I turned up there the first day and was treated like a minor celebrity. Obviously they were just licking my arse, but it was hard not to enjoy it. I ended up criticizing how well they were doing it. Almost as if I was leaving my arse in the air and saying, "Excuse me, you missed a bit."

Terrible, really. It was an unspoken thing. They knew you knew they knew, etc.—recurring to infinity.

So after a particularly successful day of having my arse licked, a young girl approached me nervously and said, "What part of Ireland are you from?" She'd heard me bragging I was Irish.

"Deelford," I said, noticing how very pretty she was, if not a little young. I'd seen her around the place earlier, but naturally thought she was one of the many assistants photographers seem to need. She was.

"Oh, that's gas."

I've only ever heard Irish people use that expression.

"Are you Irish?"

"I am, yeah, from Dublin."

Well, I can't tell you I thought much of it, but I've retraced these few moments many times since. Looking for clues. Anything that might help me explain what the fuck was going on.

She went on to say that there was "a whole gang of us over here" and that if I wanted to, she could show me around. I really thought she was too young. Dangerously young, if you know what I mean. But after talking to her a little longer, I learned that her step-dad in Deelford turned out to be my father's solicitor. She was very pretty, very innocent looking. The fact that she was Irish and had connections in Deelford combined with the fact that her step-dad was Dad's solicitor seemed to mean something. I allowed it to mean that she was sent by my dead father as a gift to redress the balance for the suffering I'd endured in Saint Lacroix.

This was a grave error. I wasn't conscious of wanting to shag her. I still believed her to be too young, but I thought I'd ask her to dinner as a treat. She was, after all, virtually related, and what would her step-dad think if he heard we'd met and I hadn't even offered to take her to dinner? She gave me her number, and out of sheer lack of knowledge, I booked a booth at the same restaurant Tomkinsin had taken me to as his sociable statement a few nights before. Actually, I'd gone there with Telma too.

Who was Telma? Telma Way was a gorgeous girl who worked at the New York office and invited herself to dinner with me when she saw me hanging around there. I never really thought there was ever any chance of getting involved with her on any romantic level. She was a great character, very beautiful and very tough.

Aisling, that was the Irish girl's name.

Yeah, I liked it, too. Gaelic for dream. It's haunted me since. So Aisling left a message on my hotel answering machine saying, "See you there."

3.

She was about a half hour late, but she looked fucking lovely. Black V-neck sweater, black pencil skirt, black shoes. Very Prada. Long dark brown hair billowing behind her as she came through the door. She looked familiar, as if I'd known her before. Like some sister I used to have and lost.

So clean, young, and adult at the same time. From the moment she walked through the door, my biggest challenge was to hide from her how strongly she affected me. She came toward me with, I think, the intention of leaning to my left for what I was to learn was the obligatory New York peck on the cheek. Never heard tell of such a thing in Saint Lacroix.

Those eyes.

This is going to sound awful, but I don't care. I'm way past embarrassment.

You can't hurt a man with a pinprick when he's already got a spear in his chest. I swear to you that she looked just like the pictures of the Virgin Mary in Irish Catholic homes.

I kid you not.

The Virgin Fuckin' Mary.

"You look great," I said, motioning toward the hostess stand.

"Thanks, so do you."

That was her first lie. We strode into the arena. All brown leather and tea-stained tiles. This was Friday night. I was to fly back to you know where the next morning. It was quite busy, so we didn't get the booth. But we got a nice enough table. She was not stupid. That much was very clear, very quickly.

This was no twenty-two, twenty-three, or even twenty-four-year-old inexperienced bimbo. She talked older than she looked. I really was thrown by that. I was expecting to spend the evening deflecting compliments of such enormity that I would find myself hating her for her lack of subtlety. Instead, I ended up kicking myself for mine. And it was too late. I couldn't suddenly wake up and say, "Oh, I didn't realize you were intelligent. I thought you were a stupid fawning child unworthy of my best game."

She must have seen everything she needed to see in the first fifteen minutes of my unbelievably self-centered diatribe. Slowly, almost considerately, she let me know how much I'd shown myself up. She'd already attended exhibitions I'd only begun to read about. Films heard about were already memories to her. And I would never have realized that I'd mispronounced the names of all those foreign artists until she pronounced them.

Her superiority was graceful, sympathetic even. Talk about being wrong-footed. Of course, I've since attributed every little nuance in that evening's conversation to her devilish manipulative skills, but the truth is that when someone outshines me, I hide my anger by putting them on a pedestal. This makes me seem generous so that when I want to put the knife in I'll be trusted. Yes, sometimes I even scare myself.

Anyway, she went on to tell me that she was from Whiteheath in Dublin. I found out much later that this is an extremely well-off area. And that she was an only child. She'd been assisting photographers on a freelance basis because it afforded her more time to devote to her own work between assignments. Forgive me, but I've always translated that to mean: "I can't get a full-time job." All the while she was talking, I was falling totally and irrevocably in love. The long hands, the direct look, the head flicks commanding the soft tumbling hair, the clear skin on her neck, the gentle slope of her small breasts.

Stop.

When she did appear impressed by something I'd said (I was now realizing I'd need to dust off my delft, so to speak), she'd seem to notice me as you would a small boy: "Oh, really; gosh, that's great" or "They must think a lot of you" and "I wish I had your problems." From these reactions I realized I came off like I was trying to impress her. I felt tricked into it. I wanted to start the whole evening all over again.

And I couldn't help thinking she was bored but acting. She had a Bacardi and Coke during dinner. A big one. I had the pork chops. I still have the bill. I do. I got it back on expenses, but I kept the bill. You see, that night changed my life. If it hadn't been for that night, I wouldn't be sitting here in the East Village in New York, writing this fucking thing. She said I'd like the East Village.

She was right.

But there you go. I fell totally in love with her. How could I not? My dead dad's gift to me and I was going to say no? No. We chatted easily about advertising and I generally tried to dazzle her as best I could. She was reserved but mannerly—very mannerly. Old school. I'd never been allowed near that before. She even poured mineral water into my glass and twisted the bottle abruptly like you do with champagne.

I got off on that.

She was very attentive. That was it. She knew how to handle a guy. She made you feel like it was okay to be a guy. To be yourself. This, it seems to me, is the most devastating weapon of all in a woman's arsenal. If you can encourage the man to be himself, to reveal his character, his ways, then you know how to navigate him, and therefore he will never be able to hide from you.

I already knew this.

I've managed to stay in the advertising business for ten years. That's one business that isn't known for its charity, and even I, Mr. Jaundice himself, entered through her velvet drapes and signed the waiver. Mind you, I was ready; I hadn't touched a woman in five years, for fuck's sake.

So she did her well-behaved Irish aristocrat act and I did mine. Irish lost boy with two big eyes borrowed from a cow. She glided across the floor and led me back onto Broadway and into Bleecker Street, which in my ignorance and to my everlasting shame I asked her to show me because I heard it was quite cool.

She took me to a gay bar. I hadn't even been in *a* bar, let alone *gay* bar, for years. It took me about an hour to figure it out. There were a lot of what appeared to be very happy middle-aged men with dyed hair, singing around an upright piano.

Delighted, they were. Not drunk, just happy. Cherubic. She went to the toilet and left me on my own for longer than I would have thought necessary. For all I know, she might have popped across the street for a leisurely drink and come back just in time to find a burly man with the whitest teeth I'd ever seen leaning against me. I was relieved to see her and told her so. She liked that. Of course she did.

We moved on to another bar. Bit more cramped. On barstools clumped together, she told me through her hands— she seemed to have picked up the American habit of using her hands to shape the words coming out of her mouth—how she'd won a green card in the Irish lottery and she'd worked in L.A. for about a year before traveling cross-country and coming to New York. She became quite animated when she talked about being in New Orleans for Mardi Gras during her trip and, more specifically, the dancing that accompanied it. She seemed far away when she talked about this experience. It was the only time she unclutched herself. Yes, even while we were fucking—or should I say, when she was fucking me—I remember thinking how beautiful she looked, but that there was something else there, something unnerving, not quite hatred, maybe self-hatred. Yes. More like self-hatred. Whatever it was, it was internal. She'd deal with it. I would never get that chance.

That privilege.

So from there to a coffee bar, which I still can't find today. Must have been somewhere off Bleecker. There were mice under the seats. While I'd have been more than happy to leave it at that, she seemed so insistent that we stay out longer. She seemed to want to hang on for more. So I ended up saying I'd really enjoyed talking to her. More than I'd expected. She said she thought the same thing, with the hands again, this time reaching as if to say *Hold my hand*. I reached forward, and before I knew what was happening, we were kissing gently.

86

Nothing too graceful.

I was half standing and leaning across a table, with mice circling our feet.

But it was nice.

I felt all the cobwebs billow, then blow away in a warm flush of summer air that seemed to close around me. Fuck knows what she felt, but I was in the bag right there. I would have been quite content to keep pecking her lips for another few hours. No problem.

Except she deftly raised the stakes with a little stiff flick of her tongue. It was amazing. Like the pilot light came on in the flue of my dick. You know that sound:

thuem, or is it *pfftum*?

Suddenly I was looking at this sweet teenage innocent like she was a cum-soaked whore. And I liked it. More important, so did she. I was supposed to be leaving the next day. But it was already the next day. I was probably not going to see her again until Christmas, and that wasn't even for sure. We both intended going home to Ireland for the holidays. There was nothing else for it.

"Want to come back to the hotel room?"

Epic stuff for me. Already I'd packed about fifteen years of half-experienced adolescence into two hours, and now here was a semi-materialized thirty-five-year-old making the pitch of his life. She muttered something about it being a bit fast and I retreated gratefully. Relieved. So we walked down the street slowly, hand in hand, looking but not too hard for a cab. In the end she turned to me and said, "We can go back to the hotel room as long as we take it easy." With that, we were walking quicker. She hailed a cab. We kissed a little bit in the back. How wonderful New York looked to me through the shimmering strands of brown hair that fell over my face between kisses.

Allow me a moment here.

Thanks.

Before long we arrived at my hotel and the doorman moved in slo-mo toward us. I have a great fear of these doorman creatures, because I knew one in Saint Lacroix and all he ever seemed to do was complain about how little he was tipped. I didn't tip them at all. For what? Standing there? So my young girlfriend and I slid past his smiling—in my mind, envious—face and strolled to the elevator. I was very nervous in that humming mirrored container. Why are they always mirrored? There is nothing more frightening to me than the image of my own image from two or three different angles. So I stared at the floor.

Room 901 meant nine floors.

I prayed the key would work. I also prayed she was over eighteen. In this country, one does not want to be associated, even jokingly, with pedophilia. And this girl did look young. I satisfied myself that she was at least in her twenties, but I still couldn't get it out of my mind that the police were going to kick in the door at any second. At one point she turned to me (we were on the bed at this stage) and blinked innocently.

"Tell me a story," she said.

I must have gone white. She could have been fourteen. I told her a story about a woman who brought back a rat from India because she thought it was a dog. We kissed and caressed, and I ended up going down on her.

Now I don't want to get too graphic here, but I have to say it because it is true, and in my experience, rare. Her womanhood tasted better than her mouth. I could have stayed down there all night.

No problem.

I came up only to see if she was as pretty as I'd suspected. She was. This went on until it began to get light. She said we should take it easy, so easy is what we took. I was adamant that we not go the whole way.

Memories of being with Pen, body memories began surfacing in me. I remember looking at Aisling while she slept and thinking, "She's back. I've got Penny back." I used to look at Penny when she was asleep. It was nice to just let my eyes wander unchecked around the smooth skin. A living, breathing picture. Strange to be touching a naked body again after so long. I was so petrified that she wouldn't find me attractive I didn't even take all my clothes off. Secretly I was glad we were taking it easy, since it meant I didn't have to get into any performance issues. What if I came too quickly or couldn't get it up?

I used an AA maxim, which helped.

When in doubt, be of service.

So I concentrated on giving her as much pleasure as I could. Pen had trained me to go down on her and now I was glad. Aisling's sleeping face wore a gentle smile. She seemed happy enough.

The next morning I said that we should go for breakfast. I got my bags together and checked out. Soon we were in another taxi on our way to a café near her place. And soon after that I was in yet another cab and on my way back to That Place. She didn't look around after I got in the cab and was whisked away.

I know this because I did.

Back in Saint Lacroix, it still hadn't snowed. I still hadn't sold the fucking house. I was already out of my mind with paranoia, thinking my company had instigated a block on the sale of my house. I thought they were slipping some money to the Realtor to restrain his enthusiasm in closing a deal. I was under tremendous pressure with a big campaign I was doing for a charity that supplied summer vacations for kids with AIDS.

Big project. Big deal.

Every ad agency likes to have a charity on their books for which they'll pull all sorts of outlandish favors. There are attractive incentives for this, though. One, the agency can usually do great dramatic work for a charity, more dramatic than what you'll be allowed to do for baked beans. And two, there are tax concessions and write-offs. But it's important which charity you affiliate yourself with.

Especially in the United States.

For instance, a charity that raises funds to help addicts get off heroin isn't nearly as reliable or photogenic or even pitiable as one that treats kids with AIDS. Adults with AIDS are no good. It could be their own fault. No, kids are good. Kids with AIDS are better. Sorry, but it's true. It's not the fault of the ad agencies. It's actually your fault.

The public.

And if this never gets published, it's your fault, too, because it means that this kind of story was deemed uninteresting to you.

You bastards.

You just won't accept a heroin addict's asking for money to kick his habit. Maybe you're right. Who knows? But that's it. Charities are as competitive as commercial companies and nowadays need to think like them.

After all, they're chasing the same dollars.

Then you've got the networks. They have a finite amount of airtime available annually for donation to charity. Which ones to give the time to? Each network has standards to maintain and are wary of letting the tone of their channels slip. It comes down to which commercial is going to make them look best. Again, you're safe with kids. So the ad agency is clever enough to pick a charity with lots of kids in it, because they know from the outset, the networks will have more time for them—in this case, airtime.

Anyway, let me tell you my story about summer camp

for kids. We were shooting the commercial on location at Camp Northern Minnesota. We were sleeping in bunk beds at the camp. I didn't even know what summer camp was until I had it explained to me. Still seemed like something only middle-class kids would ever do. But there is no middle class in the United States. Yeah, right.

After a fitful sleep, I made my way to the communal bathroom (euphemism for toilet) for a shit and a shave. It occurred to me that with two hundred kids running around here during the summer, some of their contagions might rub off on the basins. This occurred to me just before I shaved.

I thought about all the pores in my skin being opened up to all that diseased air. Christ. I went ahead and shaved, of course. And after a few appreciative glances at myself, I was satisfied that while I hadn't slept well, I didn't look as if I hadn't slept well.

I was careful not to smile at myself. I want never to be caught smiling at myself in a mirror. It's okay in private. Out for breakfast I went. The crew and the director were already assembled around steaming plates. They looked rough and unshaven.

This pleased me.

I sat down and dug into eggs and toast or whatever was on offer. *Cawfee*. Then, the Camp Boss and general all-around hero of the day came in, all bubbly, wringing his hands and lowering his eyes with excess humility. He ran the camp and was the founder of the whole thing. I noticed he, too, was unshaven. This was very uncharacteristic of him, since he was always very particular about the way he looked. In fact, apart from being unshaven, he seemed his normal well-dressed self, but in country wools and tweeds. The blood in my veins began to curdle. He risked a humble look around the table. He was looking only for information. Who was at the table? Who did he need to be nicest to and in what order?

He stopped at me: "You didn't shave, did you?"

I must've gone white.

"Yes, I did. I . . ."

"Aw, c'mon, I'm very disappointed."

I was about to ask him how he thought I felt.

"We don't shave here at camp. It's meant to be informal, but I suppose since, strictly speaking, you're still at work, we'll let it go this time."

I laughed a genuine laugh. I would live. And more important, I wouldn't need a test for HIV before meeting my beloved again. Being in that camp, with birds singing and children everywhere being so cute and nice to each other, had awoken something familial in me. I saw Aisling and me living somewhere wooded like this. Light dappling our happiness, laughter echoing around trees before we shushed each other lest we wake the baby.

How fortunate we'd consider ourselves to be that our child was not infected with some horrible disease or other.

My future wife's phone number burned away against my

thigh and the inside of a drawer and in a few other places I couldn't remember. I'd taken the precaution of writing it down on separate pieces of paper in case I lost it. I had to resist the temptation to call her. A lot.

Physical cravings.

I was in a bad way. I mean, I hadn't even looked at a girl for five years, and now it was all over me. I didn't even know what *it* was. I'd never really had those feelings before. I wince now to look back on it, but I was really in love. Or infatuated. My eyes got heavy when I thought of her; my pupils dilated when I just thought about her.

The ads for the camp turned out pretty good, and one even went on to win an award.

All the kids featured in them have since died.

Don't quite know what to do with that.

But there you go. It's easy for me to be totally honest here because the possibility of anyone ever publishing this is so remote. At least I'll benefit from it as a form of therapy. Did I feel love or obsession? I still don't know. Somehow the thought of her, or even the thought of calling her, got me through those Minnesotan nights.

So I called her and we chatted, about advertising mostly, and therefore about me. I thought she was interested. Maybe she was. At least that would have made it a bit more enjoyable for her. I can't help thinking that she must have treated this part of the whole thing like a prostitute treats the talking bit before the sex. You have to listen to some of their shit before they feel comfortable enough to get a hard-on, and they have to get the hard-on or they won't have the sex that you need them to have with you in order for you to get paid. This is what I thought was going on. She listened to me, I just know she listened to me. There I go again. The male ego. Like the guy who believes the hooker comes when she seems to. I want to believe she listened to me and liked me and, yes, even loved me a little bit. Even now I seem to want to believe that. Crazy, huh? I used to say, "Crazy, eh?" But now it's *huh*.

America.

In Minnesota, I'd been in a terrible state of mind for almost two years and felt I deserved something good to happen. Having been in New York now for over a year, I can see how innocent and silly I must have sounded to a twenty-seven-year-old hungry-as-fuck photographer determined to crack the New York scene. Fair enough. Her fascination must have been of the morbid variety, but mine wasn't much more developed.

I wanted her to help me out. Out of Saint Lacroix. I wanted her to be my pathfinder in New York. I wanted her. I wanted a lot.

I had my reasons and I suppose she had hers. To her, I must have seemed like a big wet fat bald overpaid Culchie, a name reserved for anyone from outside the Dublin area.

Ripe for harvest.

Aisling would have seen a lot of my type in her travels as a photographer's assistant. Shoots in Miami—the light,

95

darling—were commonplace for photographers from cloudy New York. Lots of hotel rooms and bars and long shoots. Loads of art directors like me with money and wives and kids and mortgages. I hope I stuck out because all I had of these was the mortgage.

She must have thought I was married, though, or hoped it. You see, I couldn't help thinking she was gathering information on me for some later use. Perhaps she wanted material to blackmail me against the wife she imagined me to have. Well, why else would I be living in a three-bedroom Victorian house? The reason for the blackmail? To get big, juicy commissions from the ad agency. It'd be worth a lot to her as a fledgling photographer to get a job or two from such a renowned company.

I thought, "What the hell, she's very pretty, I'm lonely. I'm also in need of a courage booster." I wouldn't have had the balls to do the next bit if I hadn't had a tasty chick egging me on. I gave her the power to pull me out of there.

I started calling the personnel department, inquiring about how to resign. As if I didn't know. I wanted them to know I was serious. I was past caring. In reality, it was a crazy move. They must have been sure I was in love, and let's face it, I was. I made a point of asking if what we discussed was confidential, knowing they'd have to inform the group head in such a situation. So I was able to threaten resignation without having to resign. Graham, my boss, knew what I wanted him to know. That I was serious.

It didn't take long before he asked me in passing whether I'd sold my house. I'll never forget the expression on his face. God help me, but I enjoyed it. And again, believe me, I got my version of this happening to me later, but this was my moment. The best way I can describe his pale face is to say that it rippled. From below his chin and upward to his hairline, one solitary ripple. Like milk. He was that pale. It took a couple of beats for its significance to register in him and then in me. I didn't think it would matter that much to him, one way or the other. But seemingly it did. He really must have thought he had me for another couple of years. If I'd succumbed to the Swedish women, he probably would have.

The next day he called me in to say that I was to fly to New York to help out at the office for a few weeks. I didn't know that I wouldn't be coming back, but I hoped it. I'd be able to see my Aisling. I didn't care about the job. Fuck the job, I was sick of advertising and everyone in it. All I wanted was a few weeks paid up in a nice hotel in New York with my love.

Back at Fort Fuck-up, my nickname for the house, I'd speak to her. I'd imagine she was sitting in a chair in front of me. I'd look lovingly at the middle distance just above the chair as if into her green eyes and cock my head, impressed. Nodding courteously, I'd lean forward and agree almost reluctantly with what she had to say. She was so intelligent that even I had to concede a point.

And then I would laugh happily. Because I was happy.

I was conducting a love affair. The perfect love affair, with no interruptions from anyone else. I saw a cartoon that had a picture of Narcissus staring at his own reflection in a pond. His girlfriend is asking him: "Narcissus, is there someone else?"

If they fired me at the end of my New York sojourn, fine, at least I'd have had a few memorable moments. I had tried to organize trips to New York before, but they'd all fallen through. Each time I desperately tried to hide the disappointment in my voice as I told Aisling I couldn't make it after all.

I'd kick myself as I felt any hope of our relationship slip. It was killing me. Then I'd call on Saturday morning around 10:30 AM and she wouldn't be there. The one-hour difference made it even more anxiety-provoking: 9:30 AM in New York. Jesus, my mind would have fun with that, I can tell you.

Not there?

Obviously, on her way home from some guy's flat or maybe even still there fucking him. Why not? She got into bed with me the first night we went out. But that was different, that was love. That was with me. I'd call and offer to turn up there one weekend. This she would deflect gracefully, saying it was nicer if I didn't have to pay myself. Better to wait for a business trip. She was right, of course, but I was gagging for some sex. I could see also that she was ambitious. Not afraid to talk about her work.

This scared me a little because it meant she was interested in me only because of my position as senior art director. I hated the word "senior," made me sound old. To her, I must have seemed old as fuck. I consoled myself that I didn't look much more than thirty-two. She played along with that. What pretty just-turned-twenty-seven-year-old wouldn't? She was having an exhibition, she said one night. I was so glad she was involving me in her life enough to tell me this detail that I offered to help. I tried to impress her with my talents as a media manipulator, but she wasn't impressed.

Disappointed, more like.

I wanted to cheapen the whole thing by putting a Saint Patrick's Day spin on it.

Now I can see how this must have made her more comfortable with what she was going to do. It's funny how after we decide we don't like someone, we can find reasons to support our decision, and equally the other way around. That's what I think was happening. As I got further in, I had already decided I liked—nay, loved—her and progressively began gathering and threading together a daisy chain of little observations and nuances that tied her tenderly to me.

Concurrently she was compiling her own list.

Of grievances.

I remember silences after I'd say something. The type of silence in which you let the now-silent speaker stew. Like a spotlight on what's been said. Like repeating something in a cold, dispassionate voice. And in those rests she took from me, she refueled her fervor to complete what she must have already begun.

Here's what I know about her.

Twenty-seven years old. Aisling McCarthy. Photographic assistant. Worked as a project manager in a big clunky design firm in Dublin in the early 1990s. Left Dublin after winning a green card in the lottery. Told me that she had to leave Dublin in a hurry. Worked in L.A. for about a year. Worked as a hostess in the Green Room, a four-star restaurant that catered to Dublin's elite. I try not to define "hostess" unless I'm feeling particularly unkind.

She loves Deelford, my hometown, and her step-dad Mr. Tom Bannister, the solicitor of my father, now dead.

Her mother is from Ballina. Fairly patriotic toward Ireland, but not in an unattractive Fenian sort of way. When I knew her, she worked as one of Peter Freeman's assistants, big-shot photographer, very big-shot photographer, probably one of the best in New York and, therefore, the world. She was sharing an apartment in New York's Lower East Side with two roommates. Her home in Ireland is in Whiteheath. Very fucking posh, believe me. And she looks very, very young. She's been mistaken for sixteen.

Spent time in a convent boarding school as a kid. There was a nun with whom she was quite close. Also, her grandfather died during the time I knew her.

She is obsessed with portraiture, specifically high-contrast black-and-white.

She's been in Spain and worked at a museum.

All this data retained after one short evening and no more than four phone calls. She could never accuse me of not listening. If anything, I listened too much. I was trying to soak her up into me. I could have written a book about her.

Whoops.

She went on holidays once with her family to Peru. She said she was disgusted by the way they looked at her. So fair-skinned, in those leather-faced, raven-haired sur-roundings. A lot of computer learning was required in her new job. She encouraged me to set up my own agency in Dublin. She liked to drink Guinness. She got help with her work from Peter Freeman. He even came in on the week-ends a few times to help her. I was jealous when I heard this.

That's about it. Apart, of course, from the rest of what I'm going to tell you. I will say this. I'm surprising myself here because I'm normally more cautious. If there was a way that I could torture and kill her without going to prison, I would. Or I feel like I could. Don't worry, I don't daydream about how or what I'd do. I just feel capable of doing her harm. I won't, though. These pages are the nearest I will ever get to evening up the effects of that evening in March. But let's not jump ahead here, shall we? I've been thin with rage for almost six months. To cause that kind of lividness in someone takes a certain amount of talent and, I'd like to think, intelligence. Love, hate, what's the difference?

One night on the phone, she told me she had a publishing deal. That's interesting,

I said and asked her what kind of deal and how did she manage to wrangle that? I was always interested in avenues that could lead out of advertising. She said she had some friend studying publishing at Princeton. I tried not to gulp. These were rich motherfuckers we were dealing with here. I forgot, of course, that I was making serious bucks by then. I've never felt rich. Just silly. Especially in that house. The book would consist of photo-essays, she said. Portraits. She already had some done. But she had a couple of years to complete them.

I was immediately jealous. I yearned to do something pure. Something that didn't need to sell something.

"Maybe you'll be in it," she said.

This was left open. I didn't know if I should be flattered, but I was. We arranged to meet in Dublin while we were both home in Ireland over Christmas. I called from Saint Lacroix and booked a nice room in the Shelbourne Hotel in Dublin. Saint Lacroix was fucking freezing as I jumped gratefully into a cab, exhaled loudly, and in an American accent told the driver to take me to the airport. It was a forty-five-minute drive, and no, I did not want to converse. The flight was long, too. Eight and a half hours. Actually it was more because of Northsouth Airlines.

The worst airline in the world.

Delays were standard. I only ever brought carry-on luggage, because otherwise the bags would end up being delivered two days later to wherever you were. People were always shouting at Northsouth's staff, and they obviously were accustomed to being shouted at, wore professional masks of indifference. They were the only airline out of Minnesota, so there wasn't a lot you could do . . . except shout.

I expected to be very tired before I met my loved one in Dublin. I built in a few hours to allow me some sleep in the Shelbourne before waking to find a message under my door.

There on Shelbourne Hotel stationery was one of those *Please Call, WYWO* things with ticked boxes. *Aisling* in beautiful handwriting headed the ensemble of Victorian typography that seemed so exotic now after a year and a half in the history-free environment from which I had just been delivered.

I still had an hour or so to kill before calling her at seven PM, as requested by the ticked box. I needed some condoms and began to panic because I couldn't remember if Ireland was still medieval in that department. There was a time not too long ago when you couldn't buy them. They had to be prescribed.

I went for a walk. I turned right out of the Shelbourne's beautiful front door and headed toward Grafton Street. I had to hold back the tears. I don't think I can capture what it felt like to walk among all those beautiful young faces. It was as if someone was going to shout, "Not him. No. Everyone else is allowed walk through here and to laugh and be easygoing and dress well, but not him. He shouldn't even be here."

It was so lovely. I don't even know if it was Grafton Street. It was pedestrian only, the day before Christmas Eve. I'll never forget the moment. I even found a Boots chemist, which made me feel as if I was in London. Dublin had changed so much, and so had I.

I was sadder.

But after buying a twelve-pack of condoms (hey, some of them might break), I cheered up somewhat. I walked back to the hotel, feeling like someone who'd just got out of prison. I called her home number from my room and got some guy. Her dad? Her step-dad? Jesus, I wasn't expecting that. So I just said I'd call back later or something. He didn't sound too happy. At seven o'clock, she called and said we should meet at the corner of Grafton Street at that big glass shopping center thing. I knew it, and trying to remain calm, I agreed to see her there in fifteen minutes. Fifteen minutes? I strolled there and waited for her across the road. She was a little late. But very beautiful. I had to keep checking to convince myself that she really was as lovely as she seemed. She, I thought, was doing the same thing with me, but I realize now that she must have been checking how moonfaced I looked. How easily taken in I was.

We had something to eat in a nearby café, and it was there that the first photo was taken. I didn't really even notice it, but I saw something in her eyes after she clicked thc little disposable camera button. She said it probably wouldn't even come out in the dimly lit restaurant. I had asked her if she carried a camera around. She said she did, but that I'd laugh if I saw it. I said I wouldn't. She said I would. So I said okay, I would. She took out a disposable camera (the kind you see at newsagents), and tilting it off the tabletop so that it pointed upward under my chin, she clicked the shutter. I remember I was looking at her when she took it. Looking directly into her big innocent green eyes . . . click. I immediately felt robbed.

She'd got my moon face.

My idiotic stare had been sucked off my face, replaced by an expression of distrust. Only for a moment. My first instinct had been right. I knew that a shot taken like that—impromptu, no waiting, taken by a professional—wasn't meant to be flattering.

She had water with the meal, and later we ended up in a pub in Temple Bar, where she drank Bacardis and Coke for the rest of the evening, as I downed about five bottles of Bally-fucking-gowan water. She must have been out of her mind by the time we returned to the hotel. I was pleased about how I handled that. I said, "It's a pity you can't come back to the hotel."

"Why, are there rules? Can't you have people back?" she asked.

"No, I just assumed you wouldn't be able to come back, what with your parents and—"

"Oh, no. I'd like to come back."

Ding ding. Full steam ahead. Mind those icebergs. We strolled back to the hotel, her clasping my stumpy hand in her long fingers. The evening was beautiful, and the trees along Stephen's Green were yellowed by the streetlights against the navy sky. We didn't say much. She'd been kissing me. Nonstop. There was one time when her big eyes dilated and then her pupils shrunk to little pinheads. That freaked me out a little. I didn't know if she was on something or not. In the room, we got down to business in what I now see as a fairly matter-of-fact manner. We used MTV as lighting.

It was great. I loved it. She was very beautiful. Very. I suppose I wouldn't even be writing this if she hadn't been. It wasn't every day a guy had the chance for unrushed sex with the Virgin Mary when she was sixteen. She had a great angular back. I had hair on mine. I couldn't stop giggling. Actually, there were even moments when I laughed out loud. She got a bit annoyed by this. I couldn't stop, though. It felt so good. When I feel good like that, I laugh.

She thought I was laughing at her. Also, I was nervous. It had been (yes, we know) five years. We rolled around and basically kept ourselves busy till dawn. I can remember her on top of me at one point. Her long rich brown hair falling forward as she pumped me. The hair formed a darkness that looked like the interior of the hood of the Grim Reaper. Like something out of one of those horror movies where from the darkness you see the faint glint of two little red beads.

I couldn't help thinking about how she said she'd been to Mardi Gras in New Orleans and how she'd been impressed by the dancers and the atmosphere of the whole festival. I imagined some fucked-up voodoo types smothered in chicken's blood. Only this was Dublin. We were a long way from Louisiana now, and the dawn was knocking gently on the window. I began to prepare myself for our parting. We ordered breakfast and I took a shower after her.

When I came out of the bathroom, she was leaning out the window, taking photos with her little disposable camera. No doubt we'd be seeing them again soon.

God knows what else she took while I was transferring from the bathrobe to my clothes. But she had all the opportunity she needed. So on the way to the elevator she walked ahead of me. She turned to me, fixing me in those big green headlights, and said, "I look like shit."

"You don't look that bad." I was trying not to let her know how just how beautiful she did look.

"*That* bad?" she quipped, obviously annoyed. I winced. She made a phone call from reception. She'd made one the night before, too. To let her parents know she wouldn't be home. We had coffee and I got a cab to Heuston Station. And that was it, basically.

The second Christmas after my dad died, I was at home. We did all right, Ma and me. My dad always loved Christmas, so the empty chair really stuck out this time of the year. But I was optimistic. Well, actually no, I was high. I had a gorgeous Irish girlfriend and my house was in the throes of being sold, which meant Saint Lacroix as a city of residence was nearing the end of its reign. I was a cheerful influence around the house that Christmas. My brother visited. I went to my AA meetings. Aisling even visited me in Deelford, and we had coffee in a new café. A converted bank. Ireland had changed so much. Nothing bothered me.

In hindsight, I think she wanted to invite me to a New Year's party that one of her friends in Dublin held every year. She was in Deelford to visit her step-dad and had broken away to see me. It was two days before New Year's Eve.

Maybe she had wanted to do on New Year's Eve what she ended up doing to me in the Cat and Mouse Bar in New York three months later. I have nothing to indicate that this was the case except my notoriously faulty intuition/paranoia. The night we'd met in Dublin she had mentioned that a friend of hers was visiting from New York for the Christmas period and that she'd left him in a bar somewhere. When we first met and kissed that night, there was a strong smell of alcohol, so she must had a few drinks with him before meeting me. I of course protested that he shouldn't be left alone, that we should invite him to join us.

Her long hands wiped away the suggestion. "He's too rude, you wouldn't like him."

I believe I met him the following March, in the Cat and Mouse. Back in the Bank Bistro, I think the fact that I had already arranged to see some friends in London for New Year's

Eve postponed my soul searing for a few more months. I booked a room in the Hotel Constance for the night after New Year's Eve in the hope that we might repeat our night of sex the week before. And I thought it would be a nice surprise for her since she'd worked there once as a hostess.

I called her from London on New Year's Day after a disappointing night out with my AA friends. Her mother answered. She was very pleasant and asked who should she say was calling. Hoping that Aisling had mentioned me, I told her.

"Sorry, who?"

My chest caramelized.

And when the girl of my dreams did finally fumble sleepily with the phone and say hello, I could hear the disappointment in her croaky voice. Then the nos began to emerge from the receiver in single file. No, she had to spend time with her parents. No, she saw them rarely enough as it was. No, maybe when we're both back in New York. No. No. No.

I didn't tell her I'd booked the hotel. Easy, since I'm quite accomplished at hiding disappointment. At the Hotel Constance, there's a 100 percent cancellation charge. Just in case you're ever thinking about it, you should know that means you don't get your money back.

My sister put it best. "Sounds like an expensive wank."

She also has an enviable command of the English language. And with the Constance charging 400 euros a night, she had a point. I did everything I could not to call Aisling

109

until I got back to Saint Lacroix. I really didn't want to go back at all. She was now the only subject that held any interest for me. I hated my big wonderful job. "Hated" wasn't even the right word. It was too active. This felt more like apathy. I carelessly remarked to people whose tongues were loose that I was unhappy and would soon resign. Up until that point I was afraid to even think such a thing in case they heard me. But now I wanted to be fired.

I would have welcomed it. They didn't fire me, though. Far from it. When I got back from the Christmas break they sent me to New York. It was obvious that I didn't give a shit anymore and that I wanted to be in New York. So they arranged it. Officially, I was to go and help out for a few weeks, but I knew I was never coming back. I think they knew it, too.

Especially since the sale of my house was set for February second. Two months earlier, a young couple had turned up on my doorstep. "Hi there. We were just wonderin' if you'd be interested in sellin' your beautiful home."

I had to resist hugging them.

Perfect people. Perfect words coming out of their mouths. After so long in advertising and so many late nights poring over stock photo books full of people just like this couple, I was beginning to think I was the only one who farted long, loud sonorous notes and wanked off in the bathtub. They just seemed to confirm that I shouldn't have been in this house in the first place. It was as if I was giving it back to its rightful owners.

An answered prayer is not something I was used to. They must have passed by the house when the real estate sign had been up and waited. Clever. Because now that I had finished with that agent, neither of us had to pay a commission.

Escape to New York was no longer just a dream. I was to fly out on Sunday night. I left two messages for Aisling, saying I'd be in New York the following weekend.

I intentionally didn't tell her that I was going to be there forever. I knew she'd keep putting me off.

On Sunday night, she left a message saying how she thought it was funny, but she was going to be in Miami that Sunday. Hilarious. I knew I was in for a fucking roasting. I just never could have guessed how sophisticated the roasting would be. So on Tuesday night around seven, she called me in my Soho Grand hotel room, where they give you a black goldfish of your own and where I envisaged fucking her not-inconsiderable brains out later that night.

Not to be, my friends, not to be. This night began the un-furling of events that still make my mouth go dry. We agreed to meet in Georgina's, a café bar on Prince Street. I was there early and sat at a little table. Wearing a white jacket, she turned up looking tired. Mercifully, not too beautiful.

By the way, I am aware that up to this point I sound like a jilted boyfriend trying to disguise his attempt at revenge (i.e., this whole story) as a literary event that you (the reader) are supposed to be taken in by. Maybe. But I think you'll agree that the antics of Aisling are worth recording under

111

any pretense. Call it a warning to my brother romantics. Call it paranoid ravings. Call it what you like. Call it therapy for me (and you lot are eavesdropping).

Mind you, if she does recognize herself in these pages, then that's fine, too. Of course it could backfire and make her famous. Still, this occurrence would indicate a lot of these books will have been sold, which means I won't have done too badly either.

Still reading? Good.

Back to Georgina's, I said something about how nice the bar was. Coming from Saint Lacroix, I meant it, too. I said something about seeing photos of it somewhere and asked if it was famous. I'll never forget the cold look on her face as she said, "You'll remember it after tonight."

I watched her to see if she meant something good by this comment. Didn't seem so. I stuttered a little. "What do you mean? Am I in for some big surprise tonight?"

I wanted to keep it ambiguous.

"Wait." was all she said.

That was not what I'd expected, and it scared me. *Wait?* There must be a schedule of some kind. An order. A structure she had in her mind about how the evening should proceed. I swallowed hard like someone who realizes he's in over his head. Something not good was going to happen. But it wasn't necessarily happening right now. It would happen soon, and she knew what it was and I didn't.

I couldn't leave yet because I had nothing to react to.

She began peppering me with questions. Where were the Killallon Fitzpatrick offices? Did I ski? Did I work out in the gym? Did I ever go horseback riding? Did I play chess? I answered no to all of these questions. I felt like I was being interrogated. What the fuck was this? It made me feel very inactive. She said she'd love to play chess with me someday.

I said I'd thought that being beaten at chess was doubly humiliating for me because I fancied myself a bit of a strategist. Her eyes glinted. She was having fun. I couldn't help shifting uncomfortably in my chair. She sat back and watched me squirm.

She looked . . . relaxed. Not so innocent now. More at ease with herself. Totally in control. I envied her this feeling, even though I didn't know what she was in control of.

I would soon find out.

She looked around. Crossed her arms. Then a little mannered yawn. Bored.

"I think I'll go home now," she said.

The significance of this didn't occur to me until some time later. But I did know her dismissal was significant. She let it sink in.

I must have managed to ask a question that would enable me to ascertain whether she intended to go home alone. I can't remember quite what was said, except that it felt like I was being murdered. (Awful drama queen, aren't I?)

There is a scene in *Saving Private Ryan* in which a

German soldier is killing an American soldier with a knife. The German is on top of the Yank. The GI begins to plead softly with the German, saying something like "Hold on, can't we talk about this?" To no avail. The German almost apologetically proceeds with the knife. His face belies the act he is committing. (In case you are wondering, I'm the American.) So here I was being knifed, but with bandages applied immediately after. So much so I almost ended up apologizing to her. I was in the way, causing her beautiful brow to wrinkle. How could I? The thing was, if she'd told me to fuck off, I'd have left. But she didn't. She was enjoying herself too much.

It took a good hour to get her to say she wasn't looking for a relationship. Like I was a fucking shop steward trying to understand her ladyship's requirements. At least I was able to make a clear judgment on what that meant. And what that meant mostly (if I'm honest) was no sex. So my first reaction was okay then, fuck this.

She said she'd love for me to go to exhibitions with her and she'd love to show me around New York and I was already shaking my head. It dawned on me that she had used almost all the clichés except the big one. I did it for her. "You mean you want us to be friends?"

She wouldn't commit to this. Because it probably sounded too final and she knew I'd scarper. She tried to leave it open, saying, "I want to get to know you better." This implied maybe we could get going again in the future. My instincts were to get up, leave, and call it a bad day. But she seemed to want to discuss it more, as if to hear my thoughts.

She said, "You look thoughtful," and "Are you angry?" to which I replied, "Do I? I'm sorry. Angry? No. Why should I be angry? I'm the one who came here." It was my decision. I sensed she was disappointed with my reaction; she wanted me to be angry and I took the whole thing so well. Anyone would think she was telling me about her new curtains. At least that's what I hoped. She seemed even more bored now that she wasn't getting the show of emotion she'd hoped for.

Then, without warning, a light blinded me. Flash. I couldn't see, was in shock. The guy next to me turned, grinning, and said, "Sorry. It just went off."

I nodded automatically. "S'okay. No problem."

He exchanged glances with Aisling. She was smiling. So was I. So was he. I hadn't even noticed that there had been a camera on the adjacent table, beside the salt and pepper shakers.

I looked at the man again. Something was wrong. I didn't know what. He seemed far too happy about his little accident. And the timing was too precise, as if he realized that the emotional peak had been reached. There would be nothing more expressive than the face I was wearing, so the shot had to be done now. The unwitting photographer and his accomplice remained beside us at the other table.

Aisling asked me if I wanted something to drink. I still had my Perrier. I took this to mean did I want something stronger? I was very hurt by this, considering what had already happened. But my pain was easy to conceal. All I wanted now was to get away from her and get on with nursing what would definitely be a broken heart. Something in me wouldn't give up, though. I asked her if she wanted to go for a walk. She reacted too loudly, over-emphatically, saying, "No!" and then more mildly, "It's freezing outside."

I couldn't get it out of my head that she was following some prearranged structure. I'd read a cynical article in a woman's magazine about how to break hearts and enjoy it. There were many helpful anti-man techniques including, and I'm paraphrasing here:

> Find out his hobbies before dumping him, He may be useful as a friend, or you may want to introduce him to one of your friends. Especially if he's good in bed. What better gift for a close friend? Get good at chess; there is nothing more humiliating for a man than to be beaten intellectually by a beautiful woman. You'll be able to cause him physical pain. If he doesn't let you know how he's feeling, call him late. Wake him up. It's hard for him to hide his feelings when he's in love with you and you're speaking softly to him in bed, even if it is only on the phone.

These were some of the tips mentioned in the article. Aisling had fulfilled a good many of these tips before the evening was through.

All of this occurred to me in retrospect. At the time I had too much on my plate to analyze. I just ate what was put in front of me, so to speak. You have to remember that I had a lot going on; new city (New York), basically new job (Killallon Fitzpatrick NY), new assignments. Freaky. Then this. As far as I was concerned, I'd moved to New York to be with this girl, and she was just laughing at me. That's how I saw it. That would have been quite enough, but there was this extra layer. This unnerving feeling that there was an agenda. A hidden agenda. Looking back, I find it even more terrifying. At the time, I think I was protected by shock or, dare I say it, God.

I'm sorry, but I'm going to have to talk a bit about a deity here. I prayed every day for a month or more to be delivered from Saint Lacroix. I was delivered. When I look back on the whole experiment in psychological torture (for that's what it was), I wonder if I had known what was going on sooner, would I have used it as an excuse to drink (we alcoholics like our excuses) or would I have taken an ineffectual swing at someone or come out of some red mist with her limp body held at the throat by what I'd slowly realize were my hands? The rage I felt later, as it dawned on me what had happened, was almost visible around me.

As always, I have my theories.

Because I met her at Brian Tomkinsin's studio, I thought it might be a setup. Tomkinsin did a huge amount of work for Killallon Fitzpatrick and, therefore, favors.

He took the occasional free shot here and there when asked because he knew it was good business to keep in with one of the best advertising agencies in the world. It was common practice.

One conspiracy theory is that Killallon Fitzpatrick didn't like the idea of someone they'd invested in so heavily leaving for New York, so they wanted to help me ruin myself by introducing me to a young lady from Ireland who wanted to further her own career.

She got the job with Peter Freeman very soon after showing me a good time in New York. I'm just talking here. I know it's farfetched, even for me, but I had decided Killallon Fitzpatrick was a fucking weird place.

The other theory could exist alongside the one above, or on its own, if you prefer. Theory number two supports the artistic coffee-table book route. In this version she has two friends from Princeton studying publishing. They have already negotiated a publishing deal and approved a concept of a high-quality book of photography featuring photo-essays in the style of those *True Romance* picture sequences that used to be more commonplace in the 1970s. In this case, though, each romance would feature one girl with different guys. The photo-essays would record the progression from the very beginning to the very end. In theory two, I am one of those guys.

Theory three is that theories one and two are bullshit and life is random and therefore everything that happens has no meaning or structure; it just happens or doesn't. As the man with the lisp said on hearing about the fate of the *Titanic*, "Unthinkable."

So there you have it. My money is neatly spread over the area of theories one and two, with most of it on two. Just so you know.

If we look at theory two, she had covered the early stages of our "True Romance" and even the beginning of its demise. But she didn't have anything decent. Just moonfaced shots of a man too much in love. No anger, no tears, no anguish. What's a romance without anger, tears, and woe? Can't have a book entitled *True Friendship*, can we? Well, of course not. Not if you've got a publishing deal, which means a deadline and money spent from a set budget, which you've been allotted to help you "gather material."

And not if you've already invested quite a bit of time and energy into your subject. Oh, no. Another photo flash outside Georgina's as I raised my hands (tilted upward) in what could, I thought, be misconstrued as a pleading gesture, and that particular page in her forthcoming book turned over.

The next day after promising I'd call her, I did everything I could to resist leaving fifteen pleading messages on her machine. In the end, I left a message saying I couldn't see her that night, that some work had come up and that "I'd see her around." My hand was shaking. It took everything

I had, which wasn't much, to make that call. My intention was never to call her again. Ever. I was going to use the same method I'd been taught to kick the booze. Keep it bite-size. One hour at a time. One minute. Jesus, it was torture. My ego would tell me I was hurting her needlessly by not calling her. That *I* was hurting *her*. That she had to play hard to get. That was what girls had to do.

Anyway, I somehow got through another day, and that night at around eleven-thirty, she called me in the hotel. I was asleep. It had snowed earlier and I had tried to meet Telma, but she wasn't around that night.

When the phone rang, I woke up, and who was I talking to? The source of my worst nightmare. She got me talking about some of the stuff I swore I'd never say to her. I wince now just thinking about it. All that naive shit about Tom Bannister and my father and that she must be The One and how I had threatened to resign from my job if I wasn't sent to New York and . . . oh, God. I was half asleep and didn't know what I was saying. She encouraged me, of course, consoling me with things like "I didn't know that" and "You should have said" or "That's different." I took these barely audible utterances to mean there was hope.

That's the other thing I remember about our phone conversations. I could never fucking hear her. I was too embarrassed to ask her to repeat what she'd said. I spilled my guts out and in the end left it at "I'm not going anywhere under the banner of buddy."

120

I hung up, proud at least that I'd managed to initiate the ending of the call. That's how pathetic I had become. She ended the relationship and I ended a phone call. Not exactly 1–1 on the scoreboard, but it would have to do.

Until two days later.

I couldn't hold out. I called her and left a message, saying something about having thought about what she'd said and that I wanted to meet her for lunch. In my mind, lunch was less of a commitment than dinner. She left a message back, saying we could meet for dinner that night, Sunday, "if you're feeling up to it." That fucking killed me. It implied that she knew her effect on me.

Exactly the effect.

I couldn't stop myself. I had to get my fix. I called her and we arranged to meet at a French restaurant not far from where she worked. She was preparing for an exhibition opening the following Wednesday. She was working quite hard. I suppose I should've taken that into account. I was trying to see it from her point of view. Guy turns up in New York, expecting her to drop everything for him just because it suited him to leave Saint Lacroix. A guy she was only lukewarm about to begin with. Now he was acting all hurt because she didn't want to have sex with him. I could see that.

The problem, though, was that there were these photographs being taken. Halfway through our conversation in the charming French restaurant on Lafayette, there was another camera flash. This time from a table of four on the opposite side of the room. They laughed and even waved. I couldn't be sure if the light was facing me or whether they'd just taken a shot of themselves. But in retrospect (where would we be without retrospect?), it fit the pattern. The people at the other table had bags. So what? Bags that were for equipment, not clothes. (Okay, maybe I'm stretching this one a bit thin, even for me.)

Another shot was definitely taken that Sunday night. I even made a joke about it. I was telling her how my old partner and I had been on TV in London for an outrageous ad we'd done. I was trying to impress her. To let her know that she was dumping a fucking media genius. And I ended up telling her how much I had disliked my former creative partner, saying, "He's the one you should be trying to fuck up instead of me. He deserves it. He's not a good person. You and your friends should have a go at him." I nodded at the other table.

Now, you'll have to forgive me here because my memory tells me that she replied with a meaningful look. "So you know."

And then my memory goes on to tell me that I replied, "Of course I know."

"Why are you doing it?"

"Because it's interesting to me," I said.

Now that could have meant anything, but I know what I thought it meant. And I do apologize because I can't even be sure this verbal exchange even took place. I did, however, mention my ex-partner and even told her where he worked in case she wanted to fuck him up. (By the way, I did hear that he'd recently visited New York for a wedding and that consequently he had come to work here. Say no more.) Anyway, I paid the bill and explained to her that I was on an expense account and that I was making more money just by being in New York since hotel bills and every scrap of food were expensed. She seemed jealous of this.

Money was the only subject where she showed emotion. Her lovely eyes would widen when the subject came up. So what? Can't hold that against her. Women love money so much only because we men make it hard for them to get at it. They have to massage us and our egos to get it. Otherwise they wouldn't even bother with us. Except maybe for the occasional fuck. Not unlike how we treat them.

We left the place. Not wanting to risk rejection, I didn't even try to kiss her on the cheek. I didn't want the friendship thing to become official. At least this way there was still some hope of sex. So I stood about two yards away from her (mind you, she wasn't exactly trying to close the gap), saying things like "I'll call you" and "See you soon."

I prepared myself for the heartbreaking walk back to the hotel.

"Are you coming on Wednesday?"

I secretly leaped for joy. "Oh, yeah, I forgot, your exhibition. What's the address?"

Waving good-bye, I stomped off as if I had a thousand other things to do in the direction of the Soho Grand.

In the meantime, I was working in one of the most famous advertising agencies in the world on two of their toughest accounts, Harris cameras and *Minted* magazine. Miraculously, it was going okay. The boss seemed happy. I couldn't believe it because I was working on only half my cylinders.

When the big night of Aisling's exhibition arrived and I was very nervous. I was going to meet her friends. In my mind I'm still her boyfriend. We're just going through a bumpy patch. I mean, I didn't feel too confident about it. I had a nasty feeling that I would discover some stuff I wouldn't like. I got there and the event was already up and running. I pushed my way through the impressive crowd of fashionable, comfortable-looking people. People who appeared as if they were used to being loved (strange thing to say, but that's how they looked to me: the sought-after). So I tried to find her and couldn't at first. But I could see the huge photo collage on the back wall of the bar.

That's all it was.

A big bar with a big wall space at the back. An overall abstract impression composed of hundreds of black and white photos of subway workers and commuters. To me, it was reminiscent of photographers from the 1920s or 1930s. A Russian Man Ray or John Heartfield, visually clever in the way she made the present day appear so retro.

I was shocked that I liked it so much and pissed off. It meant she was more talented than I'd feared. Not only had she stolen my heart, but now she'd stolen the life I would have loved to live had I had the courage not to go into advertising.

I don't think this hit me consciously at the time, but I was uncomfortable. No, I was jealous. And to top it all off, when I did find her she was holding a huge fucking iris that someone had given her (some guy, no doubt) and a dirty great pint of Guinness. A. Pint. Of. Guinness. I hadn't even seen one in about four years, let alone one attached to a girl I loved. Something cracked under my feet.

I nodded politely as she introduced me to her friend, the tallest, most-powerful girl I had ever seen. She must have been six foot seven. She looked like she could pick me up and throw me out the window. She had come from Los Angeles specially to see her friend Aisling. I said that showed loyalty. She said rather infuriatingly that she did it because Aisling was going to be rich someday. I remember finding that odd.

So I got stuck talking directly to this girl's midriff about sweet fuck-all with the two loves of my life: Guinness and Herself, gliding around the bar and pecking everyone on the cheek. Her boss had even turned up. Peter Freeman, it turned out, was an emaciated gray-haired-looking thing in a cardigan. He looked much older than I'd imagined. Early fifties. I remember being relieved and thinking, "Well, at least I don't have to worry about him."

I bought the tall girl a Baileys, and at my instigation, we sat at a little table because I felt so ridiculous looking up her nostrils while feigning interest in her life in Los Angeles.

All I wanted from her was information about her friend, my lover, the rising photographer. I got nothing, of course. We were sitting for a while when suddenly I felt a splatter of Baileys across my face and chest. I looked at her, incredulous. She was holding a plastic straw. She had flicked it at me. As I heard her apologize, I realized there was a droplet on my bottom lip. Smiling, I carefully wiped my chest and mouth. I was very aware that I only needed to lick my lips and anything could have happened. As it was, I had arranged with my AA friend Adam to meet later if things got sticky. This, I decided, was sticky. It was good to have someone real I could go and meet rather than having to limp out under some invented excuse. I sat for a while longer, and then after getting her another Baileys (ever the gentleman), I asked her to apologize to Aisling for me as I had a dinner date.

Happy day. I got out of there. The tall girl was over-apologetic and tried to grab my arm as she bade me to sit down again. No way was I was staying just so I could be ignored more emphatically. Fuck that, I told myself, and stepped into the welcoming March air. Superb. Within fifteen minutes Adam and I were walking against ferociously strong wind and rain over the Williamsburg Bridge. It was good for me. And him, too, I think. I kept replaying the Baileys moment in my mind. How the fuck could that have been an accident? I drank everything I could lay my hands on for over fifteen years and I never had booze splatter on me like that. Not by accident, anyway. It was too monstrous to suggest that she'd done it purposely. Too paranoid. So I forgot about it, sort of.

I didn't call Aisling the next day. I was convinced that I now had the measure of her and her crew. I'd met one or two of her friends (other than the gargantuan) and felt justified in labeling them as wealthy, bored Irish. The only types for whom the humiliation of a Culchy still held any interest.

But I broke down the next day, calling and leaving a message saying how much I'd enjoyed meeting her friends and that it would be lovely to have lunch again sometime (fucking idiot that I was). She of course left yet another message saying yes, it was lovely to see me, too, and she'd love to have lunch or something, etc.

We ended up meeting for lunch at Café Drill just around the corner from where she lived. I was there early, of course, and she turned up about three-quarters of an hour late. She only lived around the fucking corner. She even drew attention to the fact. I shrugged it off: Mr. Tolerant, Mr. Understanding. The usual banter followed, nothing really said out loud, lots of bullshit about advertising. Then out of the blue she apologized for a rather sharp remark she'd made the last night. It had had the effect of a slap.

"If you'd had your way you'd have had the fucking mass media down here."

This referred to my attempts to impress her with what I thought would be a good way to "launch" her opening. I wanted to have photographers from various media meccas like *Vogue*, *Elle*, and *Vanity Fair* at the opening. I even went so far as to suggest that she ensure her photo was good and large on the wall so that any photos taken at the opening would have her work prominent in the background. I also remember saying that it would be great if a fight broke out in front of her shot. Because if a fight broke out and she "just happened" to have a camera set up there and she also "just happened" to get a good shot of the fight, then that shot in itself could become one of the works. Also, as a media mercenary, I knew a shot like that would be difficult for any editor of any magazine to refuse. They have space on white pages to fill, too, just like the rest of us.

It was ironic that I actually gave her the idea. The thing is, of course, that it would work best if you could involve someone well known in the fight.

But I'm jumping ahead again. You mustn't let me do that. So here she was apologizing for her remark, saying that it was because she had been nervous about the opening.

I let it go. Of course I let it go. Then I said something I regret.

"You can pay for this. You've been wanting to since I met you, so it won't break your heart."

Here's what she did.

She was rummaging in her wallet, probably waiting for me to tell her to put it away, but on hearing the words "break" and "heart," she froze. Her eyes (oh, those eyes) lifted from the wallet as if they were about to latch onto mine, but they stopped unnaturally. She seemed now to be staring at the floor. I knew she knew I was watching her. For a few beats she let her eyes rest there, and then, as if noticing something on the table, she let them rise that far, blinking slowly, and with her body and head still, those eyes now shifted up and sideways to look over my left shoulder until finally making the last diagonal ascent up my cheek to burrow into my sockets.

"I. Don't. Think. So."

That's what she said. As if she knew she could kill me right there and then, but the timing wasn't right. It was the discipline that frightened me. It meant that she was doing whatever she was doing for professional reasons. There would be no passion here. And therefore, there had been no passion before. The Shelbourne had merely been a necessary act, part of a preordained tried and tested formula. Right down to the part where she tapped me on the shoulder in the middle of our lovemaking and posed like a naughty sixteen-year-old girl, complete with a coquettish smile and a nod downward at her body to ensure that I took away the intended mental snapshot. No one can say she didn't understand the nature of photography. The restraint she showed that lunchtime told me how deeply sophisticated she was, and made me want her even more.

To be honest, I had an idea I was being taken in, but I wanted to be taken somewhere . . . anywhere. After all, if this was what she wanted and I could give it to her, then why not?

I was in love with her, wasn't I? Also, I was enthralled. I'd been watching videos in Saint Lacroix (French films) for two years and hadn't come across anything as interesting as this. And there was always the outside possibility that I might get laid again. But in reality, I was the fish and she was the angler. It was just a question of what she wanted me to do next.

What she wanted me to do next was accompany her to an exhibition in the Stent Gallery on Broadway. This we did. Only one thing worth mentioning here. When we arrived at one of the cross streets, I forget which one, she spun round as if to save me from walking in front of traffic and hit me really hard in the chest. I mean, really fucking hard.

For a second I couldn't breathe. I was dazed, I'd already lost about a stone from shock. I read somewhere that when someone is in emotional shock, the area around the heart loses some of its protective fat and is therefore dangerously exposed. One well-aimed punch is not just painful; when the person who has been in shock starts to put the weight back on, the heart remains bruised, and this can lead to aortic fibrillation. It's not life threatening, but it is uncomfortable.

It hurt, but I pretended it didn't.

Next port of call on my own personal voyage of discovery was the Chess Café. Yes, they have such a thing in New York. In SoHo. It was awful. We were strolling around some of the most romantic real estate on the globe and I might just as well have been in hell. I was right beside the girl of my dreams, who was also the source of some of the worst pain I have ever experienced. In the Chess Café you paid a dollar to rent a table and you could play chess for as long as you liked. They served coffee, and true to chess-player neutrality, it was one of the few places left where you were not only allowed to smoke but actively encouraged to do so. All that frowning looked good through plumes of cigarette smoke.

She beat me easily, and I found myself squirming in my creaky chair just like I'd done in Georgina's. She leaned back as if mentally warming her hands again, just as she'd done in Georgina's. I tipped over my king in the second game. She looked up all hurt and cheated. Hurt because I was cutting short her enjoyment. Cheated because she was probably planning a long-drawn-out death for me and now I had killed myself and denied her the pleasure. Also, it must have shown her how I played the life game: I'd self destruct rather than prolong pain. She protested too much. Like it was significant.

Like I'd hit a nerve.

"Finish the game," she cried.

I said something about not wanting to prolong the agony and complimented her on how good she was at chess.

"Why? Because I beat you?"

By now I was almost limping. I was mentally and emotionally in tatters. One more blow and I would have started crying. Bawling in the street. Just one more remark and the hairline cracks behind my eyes would begin first to squirt and then to gush and finally a deluge would turn the thin streets of SoHo into canals.

I had my good friend and mentor Dean to meet at six-thirty and told her so. I was never so grateful and yet heart-broken to get away from her that afternoon. I didn't have the courage to even kiss her cheek. I feared one last rejection would push me over the edge. I stomped away again filled with rage, confusion, fear, love, and relief. We had talked about seeing a movie during the week.

I was sick of talking about her. But I had to tell someone the whole story. Not just bits and pieces here and there, but the whole thing, partly because I didn't know if I believed it myself. I thought that if I wrote it down, I could at last walk away from it all. It would be dealt with. And maybe it'd act as a warning to the others.

The next week I was busy at work and even managed to tell Aisling that I couldn't go to the pictures with her on the Wednesday night because I was being "wooed" by another agency. This was only a third true. A guy from another agency, a writer, wanted to meet me and have a chat, and yes, they were hiring, but the place wasn't known for doing great work.

Aisling and I arranged to meet on Friday night for "a drink" at a bar. I didn't know it was to be the last time I'd ever see her. I just thought I was meeting the girl I loved, just one of the millions of times I would meet her over the course of the rest of both our lives. Love was patient, kind, and un-demanding. A lot of what I'll describe did not occur to me at the time, but later, when I felt calmer and more objective.

At the time, I can definitely say, I lived from day to day in a mild form of shock.

No question about it.

I got there early. She'd said eight-thirty to nine, so I was there around eight-fifteen. I was the first. After a few minutes, her friend Sharon (Irish) and a guy (we'll call him Brazilian Shirt because he was in fact wearing a yellow Brazilian football shirt) came into the bar.

Sharon chatted for a while, and when I said I was a friend of Aisling's, Brazilian Shirt said, "Oh, another one?" I felt odd immediately, and he seemed overly unfriendly. Unfriendly for the sake of it. So this went on for a while, with me not saying much and him trying to be unfriendly with someone who was agreeing with him.

Then she turned up. She looked great. I think she'd had a few drinks. Maybe even something else, the way her eyes sparkled. Maybe it was just the anticipation. They all seemed to have a heightened sense of something about them. If my theory is right, they were enjoying the thrill of the pre-kill. Or maybe they were just looking forward to a good night out. Aisling hardly looked at me, barely acknowledged me.

Again I was very hurt by this but moved into autopilot. I told myself to smile politely and not let them know how I felt. If I'd left right then, I'd have had a much nicer evening and wouldn't be sitting here writing this. But I was curious to see if I might get laid. I knew she'd be getting fairly drunk and after all, I had nothing else to do.

My options were to be tortured by a beautiful girl who looked like the Virgin Mary with at least the distant possibility of sex or to go to another AA meeting.

Actually that's not fair, because the SoHo meeting of New York AA had some of the sexiest women I'd ever seen. But here I was, being ignored by the only girl in the world I gave a shit about and getting far too much attention from Brazilian Shirt. After about my third pint of Coke with ice, I began to get really bored. Then I got that fuzzy feeling in my head. "Numb" would be more accurate. Like there was pain, but something in front of it.

Brazilian Shirt leaned in very close to her. Too close. Close enough to be kissing her. He wasn't kissing her, but it wouldn't have seemed strange if he had. At one point he was standing between her legs and bending toward her as she leaned back against the counter from her barstool.

It was unreal, her looking over his shoulder at me as if to say, "Look at what I'm doing. Look at what he's doing. Doesn't it make you angry?" It did. It also made me feel foolish. But that was open to interpretation. He might have been trying it on. She was attractive, after all, or she might have been exercising her right as a young chick to flirt on a Friday night in a bar in downtown New York. Sure. But what happened next elevated events to an altogether different level.

Here's what happened. Imagine standing in a bar; the counter is to your right, with a big mirror behind it. The girl you love is on your right between the bar and you. The guy you hate in the Brazilian shirt is standing with his back to you and talking to another friend of She. The girl you love makes a gesture with her hands that can mean only one thing. She holds both hands in front of her as if describing the length of a small fish. Small fish? She's snickering and looking at you as she does this. You're not really aware of what she means. You look at her quizzically. You're grateful that she's looking at you at all. She glances at you again, and as she's making this gesture for Brazilian Shirt, he gazes down at her hands. And then at you. And then he smirks, embarrassed for you.

Almost sympathetic.

She leans forward and whispers something to him. His smirk widens. Her face beams now. She seems happier than you've ever seen her. She's beautiful, but she doesn't want you to look at her like that. She can see how enamored you are. She leans forward again and he stoops to allow her access to his ear. She could be kissing the side of his head. She does the "fish" thing with her hands again. This time it's even smaller. She looks you up and down. So does he. They laugh together. So as not to be totally excluded, so do you.

Awkwardly. Then he says loudly, as if talking to the other girl. "I'd tell him he's dead and buried and that there are four others buried over him. How many?"

With this, he turns to Her to check. She is counting on her fingers. Overacting, intentionally resting a finger on her lips, pretending to think before counting another finger. He continues, "I'm buried over him. I'd like to be buried over him . . . or buried in you."

She shoots back with "No, I'd be on top."

That clinches it. He's eyeing her like they're going to do it right there and then. You're getting the idea. The only merciful thing you've got going for you is that they have not done the whole performance to your face, which allows you to pretend that you don't understand. So you move as gracefully as you can to the other girl and open up a polite conversation. You need time. You are dazed. If what you think is happening is in fact happening, then you'd better get the fuck out of there, because this is some seriously evil shit.

But you can't be sure. At least not that quickly. What if you're wrong and you make a run for it? It'd be the second time you'd done it. These are her friends. What will they think of you? Or her. If they're laughing at you now, what will they do if you go? So you stay. The other friend is giving you nothing. She virtually looks over to Her as if to say, "He's your problem, you deal with him."

She does.

You're leaning on the counter talking to yet another of her friends, some dickhead from Cork. By the way, the whole reason you've been invited is because there are a couple of friends who are in town just for the weekend whom you have to meet. These, you later realize, are the publishing students from Princeton. One of them, the girl, is Irish, and so there you go. Old school buddies, no doubt about it. And they're about five yards away, with Her.

Then it happens. Slowly. Or maybe it just seems slow, like you remember it in slow motion. Brazilian Shirt putting on a green combat jacket as he picks up a canvas bag.

He comes over to you and places the bag on the ground next to your feet. He pushes both arms out of the sleeves like a pianist before a performance. You feel relief because you think he's about to leave. Now he's standing in front of you, sizing you up and down. He's holding a light meter, which you know is used by photographers to measure the amount of light bouncing off a subject, and takes a reading from it. The thing is pointing at you. He gestures some numbers back to what now looks suspiciously like a small audience consisting of the girl you love and her confederates. They chat among themselves but look over at you and your new friend with unconcealed smirks and the occasional guffaw. You ask Brazilian Shirt Now with Combat Jacket if he's about to take a shot. He doesn't answer. Because you're an art director, you know the gestures he's making, telling the photographer what shutter speed and f-stop to set on the camera. You feel uneasy. There's something not quite right about this.

There's a professionalism about this guy that's starting to unnerve you. It's Friday night. Shouldn't everyone be more relaxed? Why is he taking such a serious stance? Then you see that the light meter is gone. Back in the bag? And he's holding a camera lens. Holding it away from him.

Squinting with one eye shut tight, he's looking first upward through it against the light, then down. He's overacting. His movements are clownish and grotesque. As if he's performing the actions for the pleasure of others. What pleasure, though? He's just looking at a camera lens. He picks some dust out of it to see through it more clearly.

It hits you.

At first you think you're being paranoid because, let's face it, you are. But then you realize it's the only explanation for this whole escapade. Cushioning it in a creative distraction, you say to him: "You could make it look like I've got a small dick."

The lens he's holding has been pointing down directly at your groin. His squint becomes more pronounced when it's pointing there. You laugh. You don't like it, but you laugh. Laughing along is better than being laughed at. You think. You see him react as if to say *How did you know that?* He looks over at the audience for directions. He makes shoulder-shrugging gestures. He points to you and then his own temple and mouths the words "he knows," or at least that's how it seems to you in retrospect. He eyes you, perplexed. You smile. You think you've given him the idea. He does it again.

This time openly.

And here's where I'd like to make a suggestion for the film version of the book you're reading. The screen goes black after the introductory credits. We hear the "Dante Symphony" by Franz Liszt, the customary pretentious quotation in white lettering on black reads:

Through me you enter the city of sorrow
Through me you pass to eternal pain
Through me you reach the people that are lost
All hope abandon, ye who enter here.

Maybe Dante's warning should be written over the door of the Cat and Mouse Bar on Bleecker Street. By this time, Brazilian Shirt Now with Combat Jacket is pointing the lens at your dick and openly grimacing with the supposed effort involved in trying to see your little thing. He picks at an imaginary speck of dust that surely must be hiding your minuscule member. He looks at you in mock sympathy.

You're not enjoying this. But you can't let him know it. You laugh as if you think he's very witty. So does the audience. You know what's going on now, you think. They're making a fool of you. You're the entertainment. It's Friday night in the pub, and you, my friend, are it. You risk a look at the girl you love.

She's lovely. Even if she's laughing at you. And she is. You've always liked her laugh. You laugh along. Her laughter increases. She's laughing at the fact that you are laughing. Now she's pointing at Brazilian Shirt. You follow her laughing eyes. You turn your head toward him. He's handing you the lens. He's offering it to you. It occurs to you that if

you have it, then at least there will be an end to the whole
ordeal. So you take it. It feels warm. But hang on, I forgot to
say, how could I have forgotten this? Earlier you tried to get
to the toilet, thinking, "Fuck this, I don't have to stand here
and take this." You made a move in that direction with the
intention of gathering your thoughts and maybe even your
bag and coat and getting the fuck out of there.

But no.

There are two guys, one of them about six foot five and
very aristocratic-looking, putting their hands on your shoulders far too firmly. "Hold on," the aristocrat says pleasantly.
"Let's see this," he adds, pointing to the lens. "I'll be back in
a second," you say, trying to smile. But now you're beyond
hurt or even angry. Now you're frightened. They're pleasant
enough, but they're keeping you from going to the toilet.
What the fuck is that? You stand still.

You need to think. The guy with the lens winks at you
and the audience laughs. You think you might try and barge
your way through them, but you don't. You turn around and
ask the bartender to call the cops. You're smiling as you do
it, but you do it, and though he looks at you strangely, it's
not strangely enough. Could he be in on this little parlor
game? He doesn't seem surprised enough. He asks you why.
You tell him you're being harassed by these guys, jabbing
a thumb against your chest. He seems to be complying, but
he saunters over in the direction of the audience instead and
leans into conversation with them.

Now you're very worried.

So you've taken the lens, thinking that maybe your idea of calling the cops has shown Brazilian Shirt that continuing this humiliating fiasco is pointless. But you can't resist trying it out. You hold the lens at the same angle that he was subjecting you to. You point it at his groin and squint. You feel slightly avenged. You do it again. This is more like it. But it takes you a couple of beats to realize that he now has another lens pointing at your already ridiculed rod.

This time it's a huge telephoto lens.

This should be where you hit him. Where enough meets enough. But somehow you're okay. You can take it. So much so that you smile at him. Smile at him?

Yes. And it's a genuine smile.

For some reason you suddenly find it all sort of flattering. Flattering that these urbane, cosmopolitan people have gone to such trouble to humiliate you. Maybe it's a defense mechanism, but that's honestly how you feel. He winks at you again. The kind of wink that is the last gesture before two people start fighting. I've seen that wink before. I've been in a lot of bar fights. Correction: I've been beaten up in a lot of bar fights. That wink means the exact opposite of what it normally means. It's the kind of wink that a man uses to another man when it's been revealed that he's had illicit sex with his wife. It says in a mocking friendly way, "I've fucked your wife, and therefore you." It's as intimate as the fight that follows. But you don't feel like getting to know this guy any better than you do. You're smiling. Your smile is saying the very opposite of what it would normally say, too. It's saying, "I'm not going to be drawn into a fight with a fuck like you. I'm not stupid."

He's still holding the telephoto lens.

Suddenly there's a huge flash of light.

Huge. At first you think it's lightning. But inside?

Then you realize that it's a camera flash, and because you're an art director, you know it isn't just an ordinary camera flash. It's the kind of flash professional photographers use in studios. The light seemed to reach over everybody like a gigantic white hand and tug at your chest with its forefinger and thumb. It almost took something from you.

Almost. Afterward, you remember something about the Aborigines or New Guineans or some such primitive types believing that the camera can steal your soul. Not too long after all this, you agree. But somehow you're intact. You just know it. You feel it. An assault has been made on you and you've deflected it. You don't feel great, but you know you'll survive. It's a good feeling. You know now that for some reason they are taking professional shots of you. You don't care. All you know is that a photo of you standing in a bar smiling can't be much use to anyone.

So you keep smiling.

And without thinking, you raise the fuck-you digit on your right hand and in turn raise your right arm in the direction of the audience. Not exactly a victory, but you feel compelled to acknowledge openly that you're aware you're being humiliated.

So there.

Looking over at them, you wait for the next shot to be taken. You're trying to tell them, "Okay. So you want a shot of me? Take this. This is the only shot you'll be taking of me tonight." But Brazilian Shirt has an idea. Not a bad one, you have to concede. He begins squinting through the telephoto lens at your upraised finger. It's not your dick, but it'll do.

You realize what he is up to and bring your arm down to your side again. He's disappointed. He motions for you to raise your arm again. You refuse. He's annoyed now. Things aren't going to plan. He looks over to the girl of your dreams for inspiration. She's busy congratulating him on the finger idea. Applauding him noiselessly. He bows.

She wants it again.

"We didn't get it," Brazilian Shirt says. "Just do that with your hand again and we'll leave you alone."

This you take as victory. Up to now you haven't been sure whether this whole farce is real or imagined—you have, after all, been under a lot of stress lately—but now you know. You resolve in yourself that whatever else happens this night he, they, she will not get that picture of you.

You smile. You want him to know that you're winning or that you at least believe yourself to be winning. Next he takes out a comb. He holds it high for everyone to see. Like a magician, he holds it between finger and thumb. He deftly combs first your right shoulder and then your left. You are genuinely perplexed by this latest development. Then it hits you. You look at her. Her face is exquisite, but her eyes are glazed with hate.

For you. She hates you? Why? That's not important right now. Right now you've got to get out of this. To your shame and constant embarrassment, you have hair on your back and shoulders. You will later have it waxed, but for the moment, there it is.

The only person in the room who knows of your vegetation is Aisling . . . and now Monsieur Brazilian Shirt. She told him. The enormity of this begins to uncoil. She is out to destroy you. This is when you actually have to restrain yourself from making some pathetic gesture like punching or kicking somebody.

You will always be grateful that you didn't.

Lawsuits in the United States are commonplace, and someone who makes $300,000 a year is worth the effort. Brazilian Shirt is now flagrantly trying to provoke you with the comb, the lens, and the occasional finger jab to the chest, coupled with the wink. You continue to be shielded by shock. You want so much to attack him, but something stops you.

You pray.

Maybe that did it. Actually, I have to be more concrete than that. I know that's what did it. Otherwise, I'd have tried to kill him. And as I look back, the fact that he had donned the combat jacket must have meant that he fully expected me to try. With photographs being taken and witnesses everywhere, that wouldn't have been a good move. My publicity idea of getting someone to fight underneath her photograph would have come true. Poetic.

It would've made an excellent contribution to her book. The adman who fell on his own poisoned sword. She could play the avenging angel. I imagined the pretty, innocent face on the back of the dust jacket. Nice black-and-white portrait taken by Peter Freeman.

No, she wouldn't bring this book out until she'd finished her stint with him. Mind you, even he wasn't safe. He'd need to tread carefully. She could get as many shots as she liked of him over a four-year period.

So in the end, I managed not to give her everything she wanted for her book except a few static shots of me standing by a bar with a silly grin on my face. Maybe that was good enough for her to use. Maybe not, but at least I didn't give her a shot of me rolling around on the floor in a barroom brawl.

I suppose my writing this down is an attempt to make sense of what happened and to try to get it out of my system. Again, I wonder if it even happened at all. It's as if I might have imagined it. The strange thing is the cleverness of the scheme. I would love to have involved myself in something like this seven years ago when I myself was playing similar games. But my efforts were no more than spiritual vandalism.

This was professional.

I cut myself on a girl I'd been with for four and a half years. The half is important. I was a pig to her. Unfaithful, uncaring, and on the piss most of the time. She said she wanted some space. I was delighted at first, and then I was devastated. Great excuse to drink. So I drank. A lot. But while all that booze was going down, I entertained myself by using my story of heartbreak to bag other girls who were wandering around in the sordid bars I was frequenting. I'd lull them into my so-called web, and when I was convinced they were in love with me, I'd start to turn on them. I fancied myself the nonchalant playboy in the smoking jacket and cravat. I enjoyed hurting them. I wasn't aware of the depth of effect I was capable of achieving. I knew how much they liked me only after I'd hurt them, by which time it was too late. Correction. I knew. That's exactly why I hurt them. How could they like me? I was punishing them for liking me. I also knew that even after I had hurt them, they would continue to like me sometimes even more, because of their well-meaning nature.

It is shameful for me to say that I considered this to be the most devilishly clever part of the whole thing. The very fact that they were naturally caring and loving would be the millstone that weighed them down. The formula is perfect. The nurse becomes willing to sacrifice herself for the patient. But the patient isn't suffering from an external illness, he's suffering from self-inflicted wounds. The nurse wants to prevent him from this pain. The patient wants her to feel the pain, too. How else will she understand him? So she joins him. Now there are two patients. Something like that. But I, at least, was able to recognize some of the signs of what was going on. Which I would never have been able to do if I hadn't actually been there myself.

Also, I want to just get a mention in about the French connection here. I've since heard that in Paris there is among the more aristocratic French a fashionable habit of inviting what we in Ireland used to call a verbal punch bag to a social gathering. It's very important that the victim not know what's going on.

The victim is invited to a dinner or gathering and unknowingly supplies the other guests with much mirth. The evening is a success if everyone is allowed a stab at the poor bastard and an even bigger success if the poor unfortunate himself doesn't know what's going on. So I know you must be thinking, "Jesus, this guy has got a chip on his shoulder about this whole thing," but I tell you, I don't want her book coming out without some sort of reaction from me. I'll be completely defenseless.

Of course I don't know if I'll even get someone to publish this, but my hope is that I can get it published before her book comes out. That way I'll have the first word in. Then I don't give a shit what shots she's got of me.

I mean, can you imagine it?

A photo-fucking-essay of a part of your life. Justice? Is

it justice that I should have someone manipulate my image after I've spent the last ten years in advertising manipulating other images for money? Maybe it is. At least if you read this, you can hear my side. I know that if I saw her book and it included some guy connected with advertising, I'd just assume he deserved what he got. Stereotypes, you see. Like I expected to be shot dead in New York City as soon as I stepped off the plane.

So, anyway, there I go again straying away from the point. Where was I? Oh, yeah, The Cat and Mouse, Christ, I still shiver when I walk past it. I have a girlfriend now who lives in that area. I often walk past that bar. I don't like it. She knows all about this. She's French. Freaked me out at first that she lived nearby because I thought she was one of Aisling's crew enlisted to fuck me up even more. She thinks I should go to a therapist. Bloody cheek. I'm already going to six AA meetings a week. She's nice, though. I like her. She likes me. Let's just say we like each other. The French for dick is *bitte*, by the way. So I suppose that's a sort of happy ending because nothing's finished really, I'm still alive and fully intend to continue that way, and I'm still waiting for *her* book to come out.

Actually, it's just occurred to me that there is no ending to this book, if it is a book, happy or otherwise. It'll only be a comma in the sentence that will be added to it when her book comes out. There is a revenge element to all this. I can see there's a side of me that's being small-minded and sad and twisted and bitter and generally like the roots of a European tree (you don't see gnarled roots in this fucking country). Page after page of pinch-faced bile. I honestly don't feel like that, though.

Wait until you hear this. Just before I decided to leave the Cat and Mouse that night, a pint glass of Coke was passed to a man from Cork by a green-eyed Madonna who looked too young to be served alcohol. The Cork man then passed the pint glass of Coke to a Deelford man who hadn't taken a drink in just under six years. He was an alcoholic. He shouldn't have been in a bar in the first place. He was living dangerously. He was, after all, dangerously in love with the girl who had just bought the drink. That pint of Coke didn't look an awful lot different from the pints of Guinness that everyone else seemed to be clinging to.

That was the idea. To fit in. And he'd had a strange night. He'd also had a lot of Coca-fucking-Cola. But this one was from Her. It was special. He knew it. She knew it. The Cork man knew it. Let's say it was known. The Deelford man took the glass. She looked at him from over there. She seemed keen to keep a safe distance. As if she was afraid he might lunge at her without warning. Almost as if she wanted him to lunge at her. She stood there, braced for action, ready to flee. Her pose had a strange effect on him. He found himself soul-searching for reasons that he might want to lunge at her.

He found none. He was protected from something. By something else. Something had stepped between him and the urge to lunge. He knew logically that he had been made a fool of, expertly, but his right to reply had been postponed. Not canceled, just deferred.

She raised her glass in a mock salutation and winked a wink that said *Gotcha*, and it should have hurt, but it didn't. Not that night. Later it cut him so deeply that he had to grit his teeth to breathe. The realizations would sear through him as if his blood had turned poisonous. Like ground glass flowing through him. He could see her lovely face laughing at him.

That night, though, none of this affected him. He raised the pint glass and held it aloft, creating, if only for a few moments, a symmetry between them that hadn't until then existed. If this was a movie, we'd be close up on her smile sipping her Guinness and then tight on his mouth as he raises the Coke. Cut back and forth. Her top lip sinks into the foamy liquid. So does his. She swallows. He doesn't. She takes her glass from her lips and holds it up high in a triumphant gesture.

His glass remains in front of the lower half of his face. His top lip is cold in the Coke. He can smell vodka. He believes he can smell vodka. The Cork man is looking at them like they're playing tennis. The Deelford man is obeying some voice he only acknowledges days later. Do not drink that. He's not thirsty. He has after all drunk about five pints of the stuff already. Vodka isn't supposed to have a smell. AA is full of people who used to believe this. That was the reason they so vehemently downed the stuff. An alcoholic doesn't want to smell like booze. Funny, really—you'd have thought we wouldn't care.

But one little trick you learn if you don't want to start drinking again is to get into the habit of smelling everything you drink.

Even tea.

It's a good habit. Might save your life.

So here's the thing. If this gets published, then the likelihood is they won't publish her book of photo-essays because her methods were exposed. Or if they do, then at least I'll get the first word in, and I will have aired all my feelings about what happened. If this doesn't get published, then her book will probably come out in a year or so and I'll be humiliated or at least mildly embarrassed and she'll be the victor and I will remain in awe of her forever. On the other hand, if you are reading this, then not only did it get published but I'm now working on either my next book or the screenplay for this one.

Congratulate me.

The Oxygen Thief returns . . .

'Lively and colourful . . . will make you laugh even as you wince' *Emerald Street*

Out now.